Their exit would cause tongues to wag

Once in the car, Beth tried to forget the curious stares they'd received as they left the room. She let the motion of the car calm her; Marcus drove with complete familiarity and confidence. The way he did everything, Beth mused to herself, watching him from beneath lowered lashes.

She was starting to believe this man could do anything he set out to do. Was she falling in love with him?

She gave him a startled look. Surely not! She couldn't love any man ever again—it hurt too much.

But did she have any choice?

CAROLE MORTIMER, one of our most popular—and prolific—English authors, began writing in the Harlequin Presents series in 1979. She now has more than seventy top-selling romances to her credit and shows no signs whatever of running out of plot ideas. She writes strong traditional romances with a distinctly modern appeal, and her winning way with characters and romantic plot twists has earned her an enthusiastic audience worldwide.

Books by Carole Mortimer

CAROLE MORTIMER

romance of a lifetime

Harlequin Books

TORONTO • NEW YORK • LONDON
AMSTERDAM • PARIS • SYDNEY • HAMBURG
STOCKHOLM • ATHENS • TOKYO • MILAN
MADRID • WARSAW • BUDAPEST • AUCKLAND

Frank, my love, and our sons.

Harlequin Presents first edition June 1992
ISBN 0-373-11468-0

Original hardcover edition published in 1991
by Mills & Boon Limited

ROMANCE OF A LIFETIME

CHAPTER ONE

SHE had thought she would never cry again. Had actually been convinced that she couldn't. But there was no mistaking the heated dampness of tears on her cheeks now as she sat in the darkness.

'Spectacular, isn't it?'

Beth turned sharply at the sound of that voice, her emotions a mixture of the usual surprise she felt at hearing an English accent—she had heard so few of them since her arrival in Verona the day before—and resentment that the man had chosen to talk to her at all; did she look so typically English, and approachable, possibly lonely?

She had seen many, quite surprisingly she had thought, blonde-haired Italian women, but perhaps none of them with the ash-blonde of her own hair, and probably none of them had skin so fair in complexion as her own; she hadn't been in Italy long enough yet to acquire a tan. And as for looking lonely? Well, she was so clearly here on her own, sitting on the end of a row of seats as she was, the couple seated beside her obviously German as they talked softly together.

Nevertheless, Beth deeply resented this man's intrusion into an occasion of such rare beauty as she was experiencing, frowning darkly as she looked at the man sitting directly behind her in the amphitheatre known as the Arena.

In a country populated by dark-haired Latin-looking men, this one none the less managed to stand out as being different. Italian men, at least the ones Beth had so far observed on this holiday, were possessed of a self-assurance that bordered on arrogance, and somehow seemed to be inborn in them. This man carried his self-assurance more quietly, less consciously, and it was all the more powerful because of that.

Dark hair was kept styled short and brushed back from a roughly hewn face of such hard beauty that it was only the grey eyes that drew the gaze reluctantly away from that fascinating hardness; light, enigmatic grey eyes that held a wealth of intelligence and knowledge in their depths. Unlike other all-too-familiar grey eyes that held only cruelty...

Even sitting down this man looked big—another fact that made him stand out from Italian men—the short-sleeved shirt he wore stretched smoothly across the width of a powerful chest, the skin on his arms darkly tanned and covered in fine dark hair.

A man to be wary of, Beth realised with a familiar inward shudder.

'Would you care for a drink?' he enquired determinedly as she was forced to stand up in order to let the German couple leave their seats.

All around them people were milling about in this unique open-air theatre, all of them, like Beth

herself, here to see the performance of the spectacular opera *Aida*.

'Go to Italy,' her mother had instructed.
'Forget all the misery and pain and live through
the experience of a lifetime. Forget them all,' she
had advised with determined persuasion.

And the 'experience' of *Aida* had made her cry
for the first time in months.

How could it not have achieved what nothing
else could have done?

The thousands of people seated around this
theatre were all being privileged with a performance of the opera that, to Beth's mind, could
never be excelled.

Her mother, an ardent fan of opera herself,
had known exactly what she was doing when she
had arranged to start Beth's holiday with this
amazing spectacle.

The voices weren't the best Beth had ever
heard, the open-air stage meaning the per-
formers couldn't perhaps project as well as they
would have liked to do, but for the sheer impact
of the occasion Beth was sure it couldn't be
bettered.

And the truth was that she felt badly in need
of the drink this man was offering, the air being
hot and heavy within the Arena, and Beth not
yet acclimatised to the heat of a late July climate
in Italy. But she had no intention of accepting
this man's offer, no matter how thirsty she might
feel!

'Champagne,' he decided firmly at her lack of response, having also stood up now, as tall as Beth had anticipated, towering over the people around them, turning to move through the crowd in the direction of the bar with absolutely no difficulty at all, these people seeming to recognise, as Beth had instantly, a superior being.

As soon as he had been swallowed up by the crowd, Beth turned with deliberation in the opposite direction and walked away. She didn't particularly like champagne, and in this climate it would do nothing to quench the raging thirst she had known since her arrival, but that was completely irrelevant in the face of her determination to have as little to do with that arrogant man as she possibly could!

She gave an indulgent smile as the female voice came over the Tannoy to announce that the interval time would be twenty-five minutes; the opera performances in Italy, especially events of this magnitude, were also social occasions, and Beth had been pre-warned that she could expect to be here tonight for between three and four hours. But if what she had been privileged to see so far was an example of what was still to come then she didn't mind if she were here ten hours!

If only that man would leave her alone. But the possibility of that happening, she knew, with them both being English, and his seat being so close behind her own, was extremely remote.

What was a man like that doing on his own in somewhere like Verona in the first place?

Even in the brief few minutes Beth had seen him she had realised he was a man of wealth and power; it had all been there in his confident self-assurance. Beth had learnt over the last few years that only the very rich and powerful could afford that sort of quiet arrogance. And the very rich and powerful very rarely chose to be alone anywhere, she had found, could afford to buy company if none was readily available.

And yet this man appeared to be alone. In fact, she felt sure he was.

And she had just wasted half the allotted interval time thinking about a man she had no interest in ever seeing again!

She delayed her return to her seat for as long as she dared after the final gong had sounded announcing the beginning of the second act, lingering over the cool orange juice she had purchased for herself.

On her return a long glass, of what Beth knew without a doubt to be champagne, stood on the cushion she had purchased the use of, to cover the otherwise metal seat, during the operatic performance.

Her mouth firmed as she stood looking down at the intrusive glass, having no choice but to pick it up if she wanted to sit down again, needing to do just that as the lights slowly lowered in preparation for the start of the second act.

Damn that man!

She would have loved to just push the full glass under her seat and forget about it, but that would have been taking rudeness to the extreme, and she wasn't normally that, not even to intrusive strangers, although this man was starting to push his luck just a little too far!

She turned only briefly, raising the glass in acknowledgement, her smile one of practised dismissal.

It would have been the end of the incident as far as Beth was concerned, except that she could tell by the determined glint in pale grey eyes that it was far from over.

But the champagne—and its purchaser—were forgotten as the lights blazed on the stage, and Beth was unaware of the fact that she sipped at the bubbly wine throughout the second act, once again caught up in its spectacular beauty.

'Another?'

The silkily smooth voice was unnecessarily close to the lobe of her ear this time, Beth felt, turning sharply as the lights came on for the second interval, only to find the man *was* too close for comfort, leaning forwards in his seat, his face now dangerously close to hers.

Beth's eyes blazed deeply emerald as she glared at him with anger.

'You seem to have enjoyed that glass so much.' Mockery glinted in his eyes as he indicated the empty glass in her hand.

Her cheeks blazed fiery red in her naturally pale cheeks, shoulder-length ash-blonde hair swinging agitatedly against the heat of her face. 'I didn't even realise——'

'Ah, I didn't think I was wrong about your being English,' he said with satisfaction. 'Although I have to admit that I did wonder when I continually failed to get a verbal response——'

'Actually,' Beth cut in coolly, 'you are wrong; I happen to be Manx.' And she felt a certain satisfaction in being able to contradict him, plus a certain pride in the small island in the middle of the Irish Sea between England and Ireland that was her birthplace, and had been her home until she was eighteen years old, was still her home in her heart despite the years she had spent away from it.

Dark brows rose. 'Is there a difference?'

Her eyes flashed her indignation. 'Of course there's a——' She broke off, looking at him with narrowed eyes, realising in that moment that she was giving him exactly the response he wanted. Her first impression of him had been a correct one—he was a very intelligent man, and he knew just how to use that intelligence to his advantage. She stood up smoothly. 'If you'll excuse me...' She gave him a coolly dismissive nod.

'You didn't answer me about the champagne.' His hand on her arm stilled her as she would have walked away.

Beth stiffened as if she had been burnt, staring stonily at his hand until he slowly removed it. As he did so she thrust her empty glass into his hand. 'I didn't really want that one,' she snapped, not allowing him to delay her any further but making her way outside to one of the bars.

The last thing she wanted, or needed, was a man like that showing an interest in her. She couldn't repress her inward shudder. The last thing she needed was *any* man showing an interest in her, let alone one of his type!

Thank God she was only in Verona for one more day, and then she moved on to Venice. She had only come to Verona at all for the opera. Like a lot of other people here tonight, she was sure.

It was unfortunate that she had no choice but to remain in that particular seat, close to that infuriating man, for the rest of the performance, but these seats in the centre of the Arena had been booked for months in advance, and there wasn't a vacant seat in the place, no one, understandably, wanting to miss the performance they had waited so long to see.

It was a slightly shorter interval than last time, although Beth had plenty of time to purchase another glass of orange juice, the evening feeling even more airless than earlier.

Thank goodness she had thought to put on a cool green sheath of a dress rather than one of the gowns she would normally have worn to the opera or theatre in London. Her uncovered shoulders at least felt the benefit of any small breeze that there was, although it wasn't much. Stormy weather was on its way, the man behind the reception desk at her hotel had warned her. She was sure he would know, being a local, but she could only hope it would hold off until after the performance; it would be too awful if it were to be rained off now.

Just as the continued persistence of the man seated behind her was awful; a glass of orange juice was waiting on her seat for her return this time.

She studiously avoided looking at the man as she picked up the glass so that she might sit down, although she could almost feel the touch of his gaze on her bare shoulders.

'I thought you might find the juice more refreshing,' he leant forwards to murmur.

She couldn't deny the truth of that. In fact, she had thought of bringing a drink back herself to sip through the third act, but hadn't relished trying to return to her seat with a full glass through the jostling crowd.

The German couple were now watching the two of them with a knowing indulgence, and Beth hated the assumptions they must be making. Damn the man, why couldn't he just leave her alone and accept that she wasn't interested in him? It had to be obvious to him by now that she wasn't. Although, as she very well knew, a man like him would probably see that reluctance on her part as even more of a challenge!

'Thank you,' she accepted tightly, aware that the German couple were now nodding their heads approvingly in their direction.

'I'll let you buy me a drink during the next interval,' the man murmured as the lights went down once again.

Beth opened her mouth to protest at this idea but was prevented from doing so as the music began to play.

But she had no intention of buying him a drink, at any time this evening, hadn't asked for either of the ones he had given her, and she had no intention of returning the gesture. If he wouldn't take the hint that she wasn't interested in him then she would just have to tell him so, and as soon as possible.

If he had given her the chance!

She had no sooner stood up at the end of the third act than her arm was taken in a firm grasp and she was literally dragged out to one of the bars.

By the time Beth had got over her shock and managed to catch her breath, they were almost there! 'Will you please——?

'*Mi scusi, mi scusi*——' The man at her side totally ignored her struggles as he pushed his way through the crowd, nodding politely to the people who allowed them to pass, not even checking his stride at her unmistakable protest at his cavalier behaviour.

'What do you think you're doing?' she finally gasped as they reached the foyer ahead of the crowd, impatiently pushing lean fingers from her arm, glaring up at him indignantly.

'Avoiding the rush,' he murmured with satisfaction, looking around them pointedly. 'What would you like to drink?'

'I thought it was *my* turn to buy you a drink,' she sarcastically reminded him of his earlier arrogance.

'Thanks, I'll have a glass of champagne,' he accepted smoothly.

Too smooth. Too slick. *Too damned self-assured*. And his look of satisfaction at having her apparently comply with his wishes was almost too much for her to bear.

'Certainly.' Beth gave a gracious inclination of her head before moving lightly through the groups of people that had now joined them.

Despite their rush outside there were still several people who had arrived at the bar ahead of them, and it took some minutes to buy the champagne and make her way back to the man's side, all the more determined in her resolve to have nothing to do with him as she took in his arrogant expression.

She handed him the glass. 'I hope you enjoy it.' Her expression was one of cool disdain as she turned away.

'Where's your own drink?' The man frowned as he realised she was about to leave.

Her brows rose coolly as she glanced back at him. 'I didn't say anything about having a drink myself.' Satisfaction at having turned his manipulation back on him darkened her eyes to emerald. 'Excuse me,' she nodded abruptly.

'Cheers.' He held his glass up in acknowledgement of her victory, his eyes dark with admiration.

Beth knew with certainty that not too many people managed to achieve any sort of victory over this man!

Unfortunately, despite the obvious pleasure her action over the champagne had given her, it had probably been the worst thing she could have done with this type of man. She had probably just managed to make herself even more of a challenge to him...

Due to technical difficulties with the set for the fourth and final act the third interval was an even longer one than any of the previous ones. Beth avoided going back to her seat during this time, although she was sure the man who was proving such a pest to her had more finesse than to actually lie in wait for her there.

She was right; his seat was noticeably empty when she finally did return, although she was very much aware of the movement behind her a few minutes later when he did resume his seat. She didn't need to turn around to confirm it was him, could literally feel the warmth of his gaze on her neck as *he* looked at her.

Maybe if she hadn't been so overwhelmed at the end of the performance, so enthralled with the poignancy of the final act of the opera that she was loath to move, she might have escaped the theatre without further incident. But as she had been, and she was, she was literally a sitting target for his forceful determination.

By the time she realised that, the damned man had once more taken charge of her without so much as a word being spoken, and she was politely but firmly being hurtled through the crowd of milling people who, now that the performance was over, were eager to leave the amphitheatre. They had been an appreciative audience during the last four hours but now that the opera was over it was as if the magnitude of it all had made them realise a need to get on with their lives.

'Will you stop doing this?' Beth came to an abrupt halt, unconcerned by the people who accidentally knocked into her in the process, wrenching her arm out of his grasp. 'I do not appreciate this habit you have of—of *man-handling* me!' She rubbed the touch of his hand off her arm, her eyes glaring her displeasure.

He held up his hands defensively. 'I just thought it——'

'I really don't care what you *thought*, Mr . . .?' She looked at him pointedly, her mouth firm as she made him remember the fact that they hadn't even been introduced.

'Craven,' he supplied softly. 'Marcus Craven.'

Why was he looking at her like that, as if she should know the name? If that were the case she was afraid she had to disappoint him; the name wasn't in the least familiar to her. Not that she would have given him the satisfaction of acknowledging it even if it had been!

'Well, Mr Craven,' she continued coldly, 'whatever you may have *thought* to the contrary,

I do not appreciate being dragged about by you like a sack of potatoes that——'

'*Nothing* like a sack of potatoes,' he cut in mockingly, his gaze on her appreciative.

Beth met that gaze unflinchingly, determined to show him that she wasn't in the least impressed by him or anything he had done tonight. '*Whatever* you may have thought I was, Mr Craven,' she said in a controlled voice, 'I have found your behaviour this evening very offensive.' She sighed. 'I politely refused your offer of a drink, refusals you completely ignored, incidentally,' she snapped, 'only to find myself taken over by you in a way that was as unnecessary as it was arrogant. Now if you will excuse me—once again!—the evening is at an end and I wish to return to my hotel.'

'No,' he said evenly.

Already in the process of making her dignified exit after what she had believed to be a complete set-down, Beth was instantly halted in her tracks, turning slowly back to Marcus Craven. 'What do you mean, no?' she repeated dazedly.

'I mean, no, I don't excuse you,' he returned coolly. 'I recognised a fellow—Brit,' he mockingly amended the earlier assumption he had made that had irritated her so much, 'in a foreign land, thought it would be nice if you took pity on me and we could spend a little time together, the sound of a friendly voice and all that. But if you would rather be unfriendly there isn't a lot I can do to change that, is there?' He shrugged.

As a performance aimed at making her feel guilty it ranked pretty high. In terms of actually succeeding in doing that it failed miserably, was completely wasted on her. 'Nice' wasn't a word she would ever have associated with this man, in any context whatsoever; she felt sure it was a word he had rarely, if ever, used before. As for him needing the pity he was trying to arouse in her...!

No one looked as if he needed pity less—the man was the epitome of success. He certainly didn't need to seek her out, could have women at his side day and night without any effort at all. A possible language barrier wouldn't make any difference to that at all; this man exuded power, and that was enough of an attraction for a lot of women. It would always have the opposite effect on her.

Always...

'Quite,' she bit out tersely, nodding dismissively before pointedly walking past him, her head held high, daring him to apprehend her once again.

There was no hand grasping her arm, no sarcastic or cajoling comment that invoked a response, and yet Beth could feel that steely gaze on her back for the whole length of the foyer, sensed it even as she walked up the steps and out of the amphitheatre, knew he was following her, quite a distance behind her, but following none the less.

She would have liked to have strolled along as the other people were doing; the square looking quite beautiful now that it was lit up by the street lamps and cafés, the amphitheatre itself something to behold from this angle, most of the outside walls being intact as well. It seemed hard to believe that the amphitheatre had been built in the first century AD; the history it must have witnessed was incredible.

And Beth would have liked time to ponder on that history, to take time while still in these magnificent surroundings to think of the spectacle she had witnessed herself within its walls this evening. Instead she fled as if she were being pursued.

Resentment burned within her at the need to hurry past the strolling people, hating this feeling of being hounded back to her hotel.

But hounded was exactly how she felt!

CHAPTER TWO

'IT'S impossible not to feel the romance of the place, isn't it?'

All Beth's good humour, her feelings of relaxed well-being, left her in an instant, deserted her at the first sound of that all-too-familiar voice. A voice that she wished she weren't becoming familiar with at all!

She had spent a disturbed and restless night. Not through any fault of the hotel she was staying at, which had proved comfortable enough; she would have been surprised if it hadn't when her mother had been the one to arrange the booking. Her mother believed in travelling in style if she was to travel at all.

But Marcus Craven's persistence where she was concerned during the previous evening had unnerved and disturbed her to the extent where she had great difficulty sleeping at all, still burning with resentment towards him. A fact she found irritating to say the least.

But a late morning catching up on her sleep, followed by a late breakfast in bed, accompanied by plenty of coffee, and she felt more relaxed and ready to stroll to the house of the Capulets in the town, to enter the quiet tranquillity of the courtyard before going into the house itself and up to the balcony where Juliet was reputed to have spoken to Romeo.

This house had to be a must on a visit to Verona, and, while Beth didn't want to fall into the habit of doing the 'touristy' things, she was none the less a great fan of Shakespeare's, and her interest in the Capulet family had long ago been aroused by him.

In the courtyard below stood a statue of Juliet herself, and it seemed odd to look down upon the bronze statue of the young woman who had actually stood on this very balcony to talk to her forbidden lover.

For a few brief moments Beth had—despite the intrusion of the other couple of dozen people wandering around, also anxious to share in the experience of looking around them at the ivy-covered walls of the courtyard—been lost in the pure romance of the occasion.

But the feeling had only been *allowed* to last those few brief moments!

She spun around to face Marcus Craven, her expression full of hostility, the two of them completely alone on the balcony at that moment. 'Are you following me, Mr Craven?' she accused.

Dark brows rose over eyes full of feigned surprise. 'Of course not, Miss...?' As she had the night before, he paused significantly, waiting for her to rectify the omission of her name.

He was dressed casually today, in light-coloured trousers, and a short-sleeved open-necked shirt of a shade of grey that managed to match the steel of his eyes. And yet Beth was sure both these casual-looking items of clothing had designer labels, just as she was sure the pale grey shoes he wore were handmade.

In the broad daylight, away from the other opulent patrons of the opera, this man was still stamped with undoubted wealth of style. Her own clothing, a peach-coloured cotton skirt and white vest-top, and sandals, was much less distinctive.

'Palmer,' she supplied abruptly, making no effort to give her first name; this man was far too familiar already! 'Excuse me...' She made a move to brush past him, very much aware that they were still completely alone in their quiet tension.

'Why do you keep doing that?' he enquired softly. 'Walking away,' he explained at her puzzled look, utterly relaxed himself, one hand thrust casually into his trouser pocket.

Her hand snapped back. 'Why do *you* persist in approaching me in this way when it must be perfectly obvious I would rather you didn't?' she challenged coldly.

'Probably because it *is* so obvious you would rather I didn't,' he answered calmly.

Surprise at his honesty instantly widened her eyes, although she was man-wary enough to know it was probably just another approach, one this man had tried and tested in the past and knew to be successful.

'In that case, Mr Craven,' she told him icily, 'why don't you take heed of what has, so far, been a relatively polite brush-off?'

Although she had a feeling she already partially knew the answer to that, she had no doubt that part of the reason he couldn't accept her uninterest for what it was was because he probably didn't believe, in his own conceit, that could possibly be what it was!

She was sure Marcus Craven believed she was just playing hard to get. Very hard to get! But then, he probably thrived on such challenges. She just ran away from them ...

He shrugged lightly. 'I don't believe friendly civility costs anything.'

He was wrong. Such innocent acceptance of a proffered friendship had cost her dearly in the past, was still costing her dearly emotionally. And it would probably continue to do so. But she had no intention of confiding that to this man.

'I'm on holiday, Mr Craven,' she said dismissively. 'I have a lot to see and do, and too little time to do it all in——'

'I'd enjoy being your guide,' he cut in smoothly. 'I know Verona very well.'

Beth didn't care if it was his second home, sighing her impatience. 'I don't wish for a guide. Thank you,' she added as a very late afterthought, instantly regretting having said it at all; she certainly had no reason to feel grateful to this man for anything.

She was further annoyed by the slight hint of triumph that had now appeared in his eyes, and she bristled angrily.

'Did you enjoy the opera last night?'

Beth wasn't fooled for a moment by this sudden change of subject. 'Mr Craven——'

'How could you not have enjoyed the opera?' he answered his own question. 'It was too visibly spectacular to have elicited any other response! Will you be attending *La Gioconda* tonight?'

The booking her mother had made for her had included *La Gioconda*, but after the experience of *Aida* the evening before she really didn't feel she could attend another opera quite so soon. Her mother had been right; it had been the experience of a lifetime, and it was not to be repeated so soon.

'I have no plans to do so.' Her voice was still stilted with resentment.

He nodded knowingly. 'It's too much, isn't it? **Too** intense a battering to the senses.'

It described how she felt exactly.

It was a pity, but she had a feeling that at any other time in her life she would have found Marcus Craven interesting company. If not exactly likeable, he was a man to talk to, and she knew instinctively that he was a learned man as well as an intelligent one.

The only problem was that at this moment in time she didn't feel like talking to any man on a more than cursory basis.

'It was enjoyable,' she conceded offhandedly.

'Why don't we discuss it further over a leisurely lunch?'

Beth gave an exasperated laugh, shaking her head disbelievingly. 'And before I made this trip I was warned that it was young Italian men who made nuisances of themselves with women!'

'I had an Italian grandmother,' he said with a shrug.

Which probably explained the familiarity with the language that she had noticed the previous evening. It probably also accounted for the darkness of his colouring.

But even so, she very much doubted he usually needed to use this bludgeoning approach with women!

'I don't believe that can be used as an excuse, Mr Graven,' she drawled drily.

'And I wasn't attempting to offer it as one,' he derided. 'On the contrary, I would be very honoured if I thought I had inherited even one tenth of Nonna's charm.'

Beth certainly wouldn't have described this man as any ordinary charmer; he was something else too elusive to explain.

But all Beth really needed to know about him was that he was a danger to her solitude. And at the moment she desired that above everything else.

'I really do hope you enjoy the rest of your holiday.' She was ultra-polite. 'But if you'll excuse me I really do have a lot more to see before I leave.'

'Alone,' he said wryly.

'Exactly.' She nodded her satisfaction with that supposition.

'Well, you can't say I didn't offer.' He shrugged with a sigh.

'No,' she drawled. 'I certainly can't say that, can I?'

Unlike on the previous evening he didn't try to stop her departure, and Beth had given up any idea of looking further around the Capulet house. Besides, despite Marcus Craven's more agreeable behaviour today, she felt sure that if she continued to look around the house she would only keep 'bumping into' him!

Nevertheless, she couldn't resist glancing up at the balcony once more before leaving the courtyard completely, her steps faltering slightly at the off-guard expression she had surprised on Marcus Craven's face as he stood above watching her, but not quite seeming to see her; his eyes were narrowed to icy slits, his mouth a thin, uncompromising line.

It was an expression so unlike the relaxed charm he had shown her so far.

As if he had suddenly become aware of her scrutiny, that lazily smiling mask slipped back into place, and he lifted a hand in casual farewell as a smile continued to curve his lips.

But there would be no warmth in his eyes, Beth felt sure of that. Marcus Craven was obviously not a man who liked to be thwarted, and by resisting him she was doing exactly that.

She had been right to be wary of him, she acknowledged with a shiver. Very wary.

'There has been a telephone call for you, *signora*.'

Beth took the key to her room, frowning her concern to the hotel receptionist; there were a limited number of people who knew exactly where she was!

'It was your mother, I believe,' the pretty young girl added, handing Beth the piece of paper with the exact message on it.

Beth's brow instantly cleared as she vaguely thanked the younger woman before turning away. Her mother had probably just telephoned to make sure she was actually still here and hadn't slipped off home without letting her know! Her mother simply refused to accept that she preferred her own company most of the time.

Nevertheless, she knew she would have to return the call.

'How's it all going, darling?'

Tears welled briefly in Beth's eyes at the affectionately familiar sound of her mother's voice so many miles away.

This was the second time in as many days she had been moved to tears. Which was ridiculous when she had refused to cry at all for months.

She blinked back the tears; it wouldn't do to let her mother know that for that brief moment she had felt homesick for her cheery smile and comforting arms. Her mother would be on the first plane out here if she thought that were so, offering any help she could.

'Fine, Mummy,' she answered in a controlled voice.

'And the opera,' her mother prompted eagerly. 'How was it?'

'The experience of a lifetime,' Beth acknowledged drily, willing to give her mother that satisfaction at least. The opera *had* been spectacular.

'God, I wish I could have been there with you,' her mother sighed, and Beth could easily visualise the disappointed frown on the still-beautiful face, her mother elegantly lovely, her features classical, her blonde hair drawn back in a neat coil, her small stature always neat and attractive in one of the smart business suits she chose to wear during the day. 'You can be so stubborn sometimes, Beth,' she added reprovingly.

She felt slightly guilty at being the one to deny her mother the opportunity of seeing *Aida*, but that guilt was eased a little by the knowledge that her mother had attended the Arena several years ago. But Beth hadn't wanted to come on this trip at all, certainly hadn't wanted company if she had to go, even that of her mother who she loved very much and knew understood her pain. She had found it very difficult to tell her mother that when she had offered to come with her, but she hadn't really been left with any other alternative.

'I wonder who I get that from?' she lightly teased, deliberately easing the situation.

'I can't imagine,' her mother returned drily. 'All I can say is I would rather be there with you than trying to push this latest deal through.'

Much as she knew her mother cared about her, Beth didn't believe that for a moment.

No one looking at her delicately made mother would have believed she was the high-powered businesswoman that she actually was. And yet Katherine Palmer was very successful indeed, a self-made woman who now owned a chain of exclusive boutiques worldwide. Beth knew better than anyone that her mother had come by her business knowledge the hard way, and had tremendous respect for her as a person as well as a mother.

Her mother was in the process of branching out by introducing high-quality accessories to go with her clothing, and it was a very important move indeed; Beth had known that and it had helped to soften the blow when she had insisted her mother remain in England rather than accompanying her on this holiday.

Her mother had already sacrificed more than enough for her over the years—Beth had no intention of asking any more from her when she was obviously doing so well for herself.

'I'm sure you would, Mummy,' she dismissed lightly. 'But there really is no need.'

'I know that, darling, but...oh, never mind,' she dismissed irritably. 'What do you think of Verona?' her mother continued lightly. 'Delightful, isn't it?'

'Very,' Beth agreed drily, most of her time spent there having been marred in one way or another by Marcus Craven.

'You still sound a little down, Beth.' The frown could be heard in her mother's voice again.

'Is that so surprising, with what's happened?' She wished her voice didn't sound so sharp, but it was difficult for her not to.

'I had hoped that this trip might—well, lighten your mood a little, take your mind off things,' her mother sighed.

'Give it time, Mummy,' she pleaded softly.

'Darling, I have given it time, we all have, you know that, but it's all so damned...oh, blast, and I promised myself I wouldn't start nagging you about getting on with your own life as soon as I spoke to you again!' her mother chided herself impatiently. 'What have you done with your day, Beth?' she deliberately changed the subject.

A brief outline of her leisurely stroll before and after her visit to the Capulet house, as well as the house itself, took only a matter of minutes.

'Is that it?' Katherine sounded disappointed. 'Nothing else happened?'

A vague suspicion began to stir in her mind, one she instantly dismissed. Even her mother, in her determination to see her happy again, couldn't have done such a thing—could she? Although Beth was loath to actually broach the subject, because once she had...

'That's it,' she dismissed, still frowning to herself. Those meetings with Marcus Craven had been a little too much like coincidence, but even so...

'Oh.' Her mother's disappointment sounded even more acute.

Beth drew in a sharp breath. 'Mummy, you haven't been—being helpful, have you?' she broached cautiously, the shutter closed on her bedroom window to keep out the brightness of the afternoon sun, the gentle whir of the air-conditioning not intrusive and very necessary in the excessive heat from outside.

'In what way?' Her mother sounded puzzled now.

Or did she sound genuinely so? Beth still wasn't sure. 'Much as I love you,' she sighed, 'I want you to realise that I'm perfectly capable of organising my own life.'

'Well, of course you are, darling.' Her mother sounded hurt that Beth should even doubt that was how she felt.

'For myself——'

'Oh, Beth, I thought you had finally agreed that this holiday I organised for you was a good idea just now,' her mother protested.

'I did.' But it had been mainly to stop her mother worrying over her so much! 'But the holiday away from England was all I agreed to. Any other interference——'

'Interference?' Katherine sounded indignant at the implication. Too indignant? 'What are you talking about?' she asked impatiently.

If her mother had somehow arranged for her and Marcus Craven to meet—which would more than account for his persistence!—then by mentioning him at all she could be leaving herself open to all sorts of pressurised questioning from her mother. And yet asking Marcus Craven to 'look up' her daughter while they were both in Verona, having ascertained exactly when he was going to be there, would be just the sort of thing her mother would do. Despite what she said to the contrary, Beth knew her mother didn't believe she was capable of organising her own life, was convinced she knew what was best for Beth. But even so, she couldn't quite believe her mother would line up a man like Marcus Craven for her!

Although the doubt continued to niggle.

'It isn't important, Mummy,' she attempted to dismiss in a casual voice. 'How are things at the boutique in London?'

'I'm somehow managing to survive without you,' her mother said drily. 'And whatever it was you were talking about just now was important enough for you to mention in the first place,' she pointed out tartly.

She should have known her mother wouldn't let the subject drop as easily as that!

She gave a deep sigh. 'It's just that there was this man, and I——'

'A man?' Katherine cut in eagerly. 'What sort of man? How did you meet him? Oh, Beth, why didn't you mention him earlier? Tell me all about him *now*!'

Beth gave an inward groan, grimacing at her own reflection in the mirror on the dressing-table across the room. She could tell by her mother's very excitement that she hadn't arranged those meetings with Marcus Craven, but now that Beth had mentioned him she knew her mother wouldn't rest until she had heard every detail of those meetings, down to the last word spoken between them.

Loath to do that, Beth answered offhandedly. 'He introduced himself to me at the opera.'

'And?'

'And he's...interesting,' she conceded, slightly surprised she should have made such an admission.

She had become interested in Marcus Craven in spite of herself!

Although it had been an interest she had little difficulty resisting. She, quite frankly, didn't want an involvement with anyone.

'Don't stop there, Beth,' her mother prompted exasperatedly. 'You admit that you've met an interesting man at the opera and then tell me nothing more about him!'

'Because there's nothing else to tell.' She sighed her impatience. 'We've spoken briefly. But that's all.'

'But——'

'I go on to Venice tomorrow—remember?' Beth teased lightly, knowing her mother was fully aware of her travel itinerary; she had organised it, so she should be! 'That hardly gives us time to begin a meaningful romance.'

'Does it have to be meaningful?'

She couldn't help smiling at her mother's disgust. Since her separation from Beth's father many years ago, Katherine had made no secret of her opinion of marriage and men. Although Beth knew she had been given little enough reason in those intervening years to change her opinion in the slightest!

'I always thought so,' she sighed.

'And now?'

'Now I think the whole idea of love and romance is vastly overrated,' she dismissed with a wealth of meaning.

'Men have a lot to answer for,' her mother said disgustedly.

'Then why are you so interested in seeing me involved with another one when you know I feel the same way about them?' she mocked.

'I've learnt a few golden rules along the way, Beth,' she was assured.

'Hmm?' she prompted suspiciously.

'The best way to get over one disastrous affair is to become involved in a new one,' her mother explained knowingly. 'Never mind that this other man is probably just as much a mistake as the first one; he'll take your mind off the first disappointment, by which time your eyes are usually open. Or if they aren't, they certainly should be!'

'Mummy!'

'I know, I'm the original cynic,' she sighed, and Beth could imagine the beautiful face creased into a perplexed frown. 'No, actually, I'm not the original one.' She sobered abruptly. 'He was the reason I rang you earlier.'

Beth instantly tensed in expectation of the emotional blow to come, knowing exactly who her mother was talking about, her nails digging into her palms as she grasped the telephone receiver.

'Oh, yes?' Her voice sounded hollow and completely unlike her usual self, not really wanting to hear what her mother had to say, but knowing she had little choice in the matter. Her mother wouldn't have rung her at all if she hadn't thought it important she do so; Beth realised that now.

'Charles and Martin are up to something,' Katherine announced harshly.

The piercing of Beth's nails into her palm was accompanied by her sharply indrawn breath, although she didn't feel the pain of the self-inflicted injury until much later, just the mention of the two men being enough to cause her distress. 'Do you have any idea what it is?' she prompted through stiff lips.

'Not yet,' she was told grimly. 'But I intend to find out.'

And her mother would do exactly that, of that Beth had no doubts. Her mother had been her only ally the last year, and Beth knew without doubt that she wouldn't let her down now. It was too late to tell herself she should have had this trust in her mother three years ago. Far too late.

But in the meantime she had this further worry; what could there possibly be left that the two men could do to her?

'I didn't want to worry you with this at all, darling,' Katherine continued concernedly. 'But I didn't want them to just drop something else on you without warning.'

After what had already been done to her Beth knew this concern was merited; together Martin and Charles could be absolutely ruthless.

'I'm glad of the warning,' she reassured her mother. 'Although I don't think it's enough to bring me back to England just yet.' She didn't feel up to returning to England to face yet more of the two men's cruelty.

'Of course not.' Her mother sounded scandalised that she should even have considered doing such a thing. 'You can rely on me to look after your interests here.'

Beth knew that she could, that her mother bore no grudge for that time three years ago when Beth had completely ignored her advice, when her mother had tried to help her see a truth she hadn't wanted to see. Her mother wasn't the type to say 'I told you so' and just leave her alone in her misery.

She had cursed herself a million times for not listening to her mother all that time ago when she had tried to warn her about Martin, had tried to help her see the true man behind the charm he had showed her. A truth she had chosen not to believe because she was blinded by love for the man.

That blindness had cost her dearly over the last year.

Would probably continue to do so...

CHAPTER THREE

VENICE: one of the most beautiful cities in the world. What a pity it was slowly sinking into oblivion.

Although at this moment in time that wasn't apparent; Venice was everything Beth had ever heard it claimed to be. And more.

She had been slightly sceptical about her mother's choice of Venice as her second port of call, romance being the last thing she wanted to feel. But Beth had felt the magic of the place the moment she stepped out of the airport in search of the water taxi that would take her to her hotel. It was everything she had ever thought it would be, bustling, overcrowded, over-commercialised, and yet somehow the mystique and magic of the place managed to captivate the senses in spite of this.

Her hotel, the Danieli, had done a lot to add to the charm of her visit; her mother had really spoilt her with her choice of hotels this time. Of course, Beth had heard of the Danieli before this visit, knew it had once been a beautiful palace owned by the Danieli family, the building itself magnificent in construction, the décor and furnishings chosen accordingly.

And to add to the charm of the place Beth's room overlooked the lagoon, the view from her balcony one of the bustling activity on the water itself as it entered the Grand Canal. Beth had spent the first couple of hours after her arrival just sitting on the balcony watching the toing and froing of the water traffic, amazed at the variety of craft, from the numerous gondolas to a cruise ship that somehow navigated the narrow water.

She had finally ventured out of the hotel in the afternoon, crossing the bridge close to the hotel before she realised that the people gathered on the bridge were actually looking at something. A step back had revealed the famous Bridge of Sighs.

Beth could hardly believe it. There was history wherever she looked, the Doge's Palace and St Mark's Square just around the corner.

It was all too much at once, numbing the senses, and Beth decided she would be better waiting until the following day before exploring further, so she started back towards the hotel, pausing to look at the stalls of the street-vendors. Here were the usual tacky touristy things that could be found at any seaside town in England, and yet even this was merely another added charm to Venice.

But the bride and groom stepping into the gondola were, Beth felt, taking the romantic image of the place too far!

The bride wore a floating white gown, her veil long and trailing behind her, her hair dark, her face achingly lovely, the groom dark and good-looking, having eyes only for his bride as the wedding party waved them on their way down the Grand Canal.

'Beautiful, isn't it?' drawled a mocking voice.

Beth closed her eyes as she swayed, but the gondola bobbing up and down with the bride and groom gazing ecstatically into each other's eyes was still in front of her as she opened her eyes, the noise of chattering people still bombarding her ears.

And yet she had heard that voice, she knew she hadn't dreamt it. She didn't even know why she had felt that initial surprise; she was being hounded, she knew that now.

She was perfectly in control by the time she turned to face Marcus Craven, calmly looking up at him as he stood so relaxed and handsome, one hand thrust casually into the pocket of the black trousers he wore, the short-sleeved cream shirt revealing the olive tone to his skin where the shirt was unbuttoned at his throat. He looked strong and very male—and magnetically alive!

'Actually,' Beth drawled drily, 'I was just thinking it was overplaying the romantic image of Venice just a touch too much.'

His eyes gleamed with shared amusement. 'You don't seem surprised to see me.'

She arched blonde brows. 'Should I be?'

Inside she was furious at being in his company once again, all sorts of questions and suspicions filling her mind. What was he doing in Venice?

On the very same day she too had come here. *Was* he following her? If so, why? She really couldn't believe in this much of a coincidence.

And yet what possible reason could he *have* for wanting to follow her?

He certainly couldn't be after any money he thought she might have; he looked much wealthier himself than she would ever dream of being. Unless it was just a 'look'. Gigolos hardly looked like beggars, or they wouldn't have the opportunity to meet those rich and desperate woman that they preyed on so easily. Even so, she very much doubted that that explanation was true of this man...

'*You* don't seem surprised to see me again, Mr Craven,' she added pointedly.

'Should I be?' he returned just as smoothly.

Beth's mouth tightened; she wasn't about to carry on a ridiculously childish conversation with this man, would rather not be talking to him at all! 'Obviously not,' she bit out tartly.

Marcus Craven shrugged, turning to look at the fast-receding gondola carrying the bride and groom, the wedding party having dissipated at their departure. 'What did you mean by your remark about them just now?' He nodded in their direction. 'It's quite common for the "happy couple" to leave that way.'

She shook her head. 'You aren't telling me that was for real?'

'Of course it was real,' he mocked lightly. 'Did you think it was just put on for the tourists?'

Delicate colour darkened her cheeks. 'As a matter of fact, yes,' she admitted tersely, feeling rather foolish for her supposition in the face of his obvious amusement. But the vision of the bride and groom sailing off into the distance in a gondola had just seemed too pat, too unreal. Did people really have weddings like that in Venice? If she thought about it logically then there was no other way for the happy couple to make their departure. How utterly charming, and yes—romantic . . .

Marcus Craven was watching her every expression. 'Don't worry,' he drawled at her softened expression. 'It has this effect on most people.'

But not on her; she was the last person to be affected by such romantic nonsense!

She gave him a cold look. 'If it's traditional . . .' she dismissed scathingly. 'I won't say it was nice to see you again, Mr Craven, because it——'

'Wasn't,' he finished drily, his eyes warm with humour. 'Maybe I can walk you back to your hotel?' he offered lightly.

Considering it was only a few yards away that would be a waste of time, but Beth didn't particularly want to reveal to him where she was staying. If he didn't already know! She was positive that their having met again in this way was no coincidence. That bothered her in a niggling way, like an irritant that couldn't be shaken off.

'That won't be necessary,' she refused abruptly.

'It's no trouble.' His gaze gently mocked her.

'I didn't for one moment believe it was,' Beth snapped, coming to the end of her patience. 'You seem to have a lot of spare time on your hands to do just as you like; some of us aren't so lucky.'

Dark brows rose curiously. 'Are you over here to work?'

Her mouth firmed. 'Not exactly,' she avoided; visiting her mother's boutique while in Venice was merely saving her mother the trip later in the year, not exactly working herself. 'Are you here on business or pleasure, Mr Craven?'

'If I'm truthful I'm not really sure any more,' he bit out tersely, seeming to relax with effort, although some of the tension remained in the smile he gave. 'But let's not think about that,' he dismissed. 'If you don't wish to return to your hotel just yet maybe we could have a cool drink somewhere instead?'

Persistent didn't even begin to describe this man, Beth realised wearily. Why her? That was what she still didn't understand.

She had never been led to believe that her looks were such that they would cause a man to be this insistent, and she was well aware of the fact that at the moment she didn't look her best anyway, her face and body too thin rather than fashionably so. Not that it seemed to have deterred this man!

'Mr Craven——'

'Marcus, please,' he cut in smoothly.

Leaving her little choice but to reciprocate! 'Beth,' she supplied abruptly, far from pleased at this continued invasion of her privacy.

His gaze lingered on the delicacy of her face. 'Its pure simplicity and beauty suit you,' he said slowly.

Beth had never thought about it one way or the other—it was just her name.

'Tell me,' he frowned. 'Where do you live on the Isle of Man?'

It was such a sudden change of subject that she could only blink up at him.

'You said you're Manx,' he reminded at her silence.

In self-defence, she remembered! 'I am,' she acknowledged shortly. 'But I haven't lived on the island for several years,' she admitted with regret. 'I live in London now.'

His mouth twisted. 'Of course.'

Why 'of course'? She actually wasn't that impressed with living in London any more; in fact one of the things she had come away to decide was whether or not she should move back to the home of her childhood. She had been very reluctant to come to any major decisions while feeling so unsettled within herself, but she certainly wasn't being given any time to just sit and contemplate the problem with this man constantly about!

'It suits me for the moment,' she dismissed offhandedly. 'Now I really would like to go back to my hotel.'

Marcus nodded. 'I'll walk with you.'

She turned to him, her eyes blazing. 'I've said that isn't necessary!'

His mouth twisted derisively. 'I'm going back there myself anyway.'

Beth looked up at him searchingly, seeing the truth of what he said in his eyes; he was staying at the Danieli, and knew she was too!

She was starting to long for the impersonality and anonymity that existed in London, was literally being driven out of Italy by this man!

'Suit yourself,' she said ungraciously, turning to walk towards the salmon-pink and white building that faced across the lagoon a few yards away.

'I usually do,' he murmured softly at her side as he managed to keep up with her despite her brisk pace.

Beth didn't doubt that for a moment. Accustomed to dealing with arrogance at its worst, even she found this man incredible in his forcefulness. He took her breath away!

It was cool and elegant inside the hotel, uncrowded, the reception staff looking at them enquiringly as they approached the stairs. Marcus Craven gave a dismissive nod in their direction, and Beth felt fresh irritation at what was obviously a linking of them together.

She moved purposefully to the lift once they had ascended the stairs, realising as she did so that Marcus Craven was no longer accompanying her. She turned with raised brows.

'My room is on this floor,' he explained drily. 'I managed to get a cancellation.'

Beth's hand stopped in the action of pressing the button for the lift, and she gave a perplexed frown. 'Your decision to come to Venice was an—impulsive one?'

His mouth twisted. 'You could say that.'

She drew in a sharp breath. 'I just did,' she bit out slowly, having the strange feeling that *she* had been instrumental in his making that impulsive decision. But why? It seemed a very odd thing for someone to do on the basis of two unwelcome meetings in Verona. Surely even this man wasn't arrogant enough to behave in that way? She couldn't believe he would find any woman attractive enough to follow around the country.

'So you did,' he mocked.

'Yes,' she acknowledged curtly, very disturbed by the thought of this man following her anywhere.

'Perhaps we could have dinner together this evening?' He raised dark brows enquiringly.

Hounded didn't quite describe the way this man made her feel; haunted was more like it!

'I'm not sure of my plans yet,' she evaded.

'Of course not.' He gave a taunting smile. 'You know, I'll start to get a complex if you continue to give the impression you would rather avoid my company.'

'Was it only an impression?' Beth drawled. 'And here was I thinking it was fact; how silly of me!'

His smile seemed to widen in spite of himself. 'You could be very good for me.' He gave a rueful shake of his head, his smile self-derisive now.

'Then it's a pity you'll never have the chance to find that out,' she dismissed.

His soft laugh was echoing around the tall-ceilinged hallway as she stepped into the lift.

Somehow Beth had a feeling she had just made him all the more interested. And determined. And goodness knew how effective that was going to be!

She moved restlessly about her room. The most sensible thing to do would be to cut this holiday short and go home.

The most sensible thing to do, maybe, to avoid Marcus Craven, but it wasn't what she was going to do, for several reasons that made just as much sense. For one, she wasn't going to run away from anything or anyone. For two, she didn't have to spend time with anyone she didn't want to, no matter how persistent they were. And three, she had no guarantee that he wouldn't follow her back to England and continue to be harassingly annoying! It was the latter reason that made a complete nonsense of fleeing Venice.

Nevertheless, she needed to hear the sound of a reassuring voice.

'Beth!' her mother greeted warmly as she accepted the call into her office. 'How's Venice?'

'Magical,' she admitted ruefully. 'I didn't believe it could possibly live up to its reputation, but it does. And more so.' She went on to tell her mother about the wedding party.

'It sounds wonderful, darling,' her mother enthused, and Beth could picture her as she sat behind her glass and chromium desk, all elegant efficiency in one of her tailored suits. 'Actually, I'm glad you called,' she added eagerly. 'Charles and I are having dinner this evening, so I should know more about what he and Martin are up to after that.'

Beth had to hand it to her mother; she wasted no time in pursuing a course of action once she had made up her mind, even if it meant spending time with a man she despised above all others.

Beth's father.

Charles Palmer had seen the woman he wanted for himself twenty-five years ago, had wooed her and won her, married her, and from that day on had treated her just like any other business asset he possessed!

He had been disappointed when their first child was a girl, had wanted to instantly try again for the son he wanted to succeed him, hadn't believed Katherine when she had informed him that she refused to be a com plete wife to him until he started showing her some respect as a person, had been sure she would soon tire of this attitude. But Katherine's stubbornness had outlasted his irritation, and the irritation had quickly turned to anger, the anger to fury, until Charles had demanded she come to her senses. Katherine's answer to that had been to pack her own and Beth's belongings and transport them both back to the Isle of Man.

Charles had followed them, alternately threatening and then cajoling, all to no avail because the man didn't have an ounce of real tenderness in him, only ambition, as Katherine had ultimately had to realise and accept.

A divorce had been out of the question as far as Charles was concerned; he had no intention of handing over any of his money or assets to an ex-wife and daughter, and after the lesson Katherine had learnt from him, so painfully, about love and marriage, she had felt no interest in ever marrying again either. But she had learnt more than pain from her marriage; had eventually used that knowledge to become a successful businesswoman in her own right, much to Charles's annoyance. It would have pleased him much more if Katherine had finally had to go to him for financial help at least.

So although the relationship between her parents was strained they had continued to keep in touch, mainly because Katherine felt Charles should know something of his daughter, even if he wasn't particularly interested. It might have saved Beth a lot of heartache if her parents had never spoken to each other again!

But that wasn't really being fair to her mother; any mistakes she herself might have made had been by her own decisions, and no one else's.

She just hadn't realised that her father, after years of separation from his wife, had given up all idea of ever having the son he wanted to succeed him and decided that the daughter he did have could be an asset after all. Her mother had tried to warn her, but after years of being ignored by her father Beth had just been so overwhelmed by this sudden interest in her when she was twenty-one that she hadn't seen the danger in it until it was too late.

But the last three years had given her a healthy respect for her mother's suspicions where Charles Palmer was concerned; her mother obviously knew him better than anyone else.

'Be careful, Mummy,' she warned concernedly.

'I ceased being terrified of Charles years ago,' her mother scorned. 'He has one weakness: this empire he's built up with Sean Carlisle. And one day it's going to destroy him.'

'I doubt it,' Beth said drily from experience. 'And if you're only having dinner with him for my sake don't bother; there's nothing left that he can do to hurt me.' That last was said without bitterness, it was merely a statement of fact. She *couldn't* be hurt by anything else her father did.

'I want to know what he's up to.' The frown could be heard in her mother's voice. 'Besides, I've chosen to have dinner at the most expensive restaurant in town; there's nothing I enjoy more than watching your father pay out some of his precious money!' she added with relish.

Beth gave a rueful smile. Her mother had lived with the strange situation of her marriage for so long now that neither that nor Charles himself bothered her any more. Beth's own pain at his hands was still too new, too raw, for her to think of him with anything less than a shudder.

'I'll call you again as soon as I know anything, darling,' her mother continued briskly. 'In the meantime, enjoy Venice.'

It was only once Beth had rung off that she realised she hadn't told her mother about Marcus Craven being in Venice too. But perhaps that was just as well; her mother wouldn't leave the subject alone if she did know about it.

Dinner on the terrace restaurant of the Danieli Hotel had to be another experience Beth would remember for a lifetime.

The lagoon and the Grand Canal were all brightly lit beneath her, crafts of all kinds still bobbing about on the water, gondolas silhouetted against the sunset.

Beth felt all her tension leave her at the calm tranquillity of the beauty spread out before her, surrounded by unhurried elegance as she was, a glass of cooled white wine in front of her as she perused the menu. She had been so enthralled by the quiet beauty around her that she hadn't even glanced at the menu yet.

And when the shadow fell across her from behind she didn't even blink, looking calmly up at Marcus Craven. 'Not even you can spoil my enjoyment of this special moment,' she told him placidly.

'I'm glad.' He sat down opposite her at the table, dressed in a dark evening suit again tonight, his shirt showing up very white against the tan he was quickly acquiring, nodding acceptance as the wine waiter came over to pour him a glass of wine from the bottle Beth had ordered.

'Be my guest,' she derided, still calm, too relaxed to feel upset by him just now.

'Actually,' he murmured softly, sitting forwards so that his face was only inches away from her own, 'you're *my* guest; I booked this table for the two of us earlier.'

She couldn't even feel surprise at that; it was what she should have expected from his arrogance. She couldn't feel anger either, was completely mellowed by her surroundings.

'Have you decided what you would like to eat?' He indicated the menu in front of her.

'I'm really not that hungry,' she dismissed, turning back to look over the lagoon.

She was rarely hungry nowadays—that was why her weight had fallen to a ridiculously low level, why her mother always fed her the most fattening things she could think of when Beth went to her apartment for dinner.

'I'll just have a salad,' she shrugged, putting the menu down.

Marcus gave her a derisive glance before turning to the waiter who stood quietly at her side, ordering their meal in perfect Italian, a new respect for him having entered the waiter's eyes before he left the table.

'I see you learnt some useful things off your Italian grandmother too,' Beth drawled, although she had a feeling this man had needed to be taught little in his adult life, that he knew most things instinctively.

'Nonna was always very proud of her heritage.' The grey eyes were unseeing, his focus inward, on memories that were for him alone.

From his use of the past tense Beth realised his grandmother must be dead. And that Marcus had obviously loved her very much. It gave her a personal insight into this man she would rather not have had, into a vulnerability she would rather not have been privy to.

Fortunately their first course arrived at that moment, making it unnecessary for her to pass any further comment on the subject. Not that she knew what to say anyway. After all, she couldn't really express sympathy for the loss of someone she hadn't known to someone she barely knew.

Marcus had chosen a salad as a starter, a glorious concoction, and Beth enjoyed every mouthful. She was mellowed enough, felt gracious enough, to tell Marcus so.

'Thank you.' He gave a teasing smile.

He looked years younger when he smiled like that, his eyes glowing like molten steel.

And she might just have had a sip too much wine on a relatively empty stomach! What other

reason could there be for her actually enjo
his company?

This wouldn't do at all; a man like this would
see her apparent pleasantness as a definite en-
couragement. The magic of Venice would have
to be resisted if she were to continue showing
resistance to Marcus Craven.

But it was difficult, very difficult. She felt sure
stronger women than her had been unable to
resist Venice by moonlight, and her pleasure was
enhanced by the unobtrusive service of the
Danieli staff, the refilling of her wine glass
without her even realising it had been done, the
warmth of the gentle breeze in her hair, and all
the time Marcus talked to her warmly about the
wonders of the city. He assured her that St
Mark's Square was just across the Bridge of Sighs
and around the corner, that she had to go there,
that they could even stroll through the square
after their meal if she would like that.

A stroll in the moonlight, through the square
reputed to have half a dozen or more outside
cafés, most with live music of some kind, the sort
of music for lovers to gaze into each other's eyes.

It definitely wasn't for her!

'I don't think so, thank you,' she refused
politely. 'In fact...' she looked at the slender
watch on her wrist '...I think it is time I went
back to my room—it's been a long day.'

Marcus gave her a chiding look. 'You don't
look tired.'

'Appearances can be deceptive,' she returned firmly.

He sat back in his chair, his face suddenly in shadow. 'Yes,' he answered curtly. 'If you've finished your coffee...?' He indicated the empty cup in front of her.

Beth eyed him uncertainly. Why had his mood suddenly changed? She had been nowhere near as dismissive as in the past, and yet this time he had accepted it without question.

And she was disappointed. No, she wasn't disappointed, she was just surprised, that was all.

But she had been right about his intelligence, had enjoyed his company in spite of herself.

She looked at him questioningly as they stepped into the lift and he pressed the button for her floor rather than his own.

'I always see a lady home after I've spent the evening with her,' he drawled.

Always? she thought cynically. She doubted very much that all his ladies returned to their own home at the end of an evening spent in his company!

She turned to him outside her room. 'Thank you for dinner.'

'You're welcome,' he returned softly. 'Tomorrow. Let me show you Venice.'

'I——' She broke off gratefully as the telephone could be heard ringing inside her room. 'I have to go,' she told him with some relief.

'Yes,' he acknowledged impatiently, the annoyance in his eyes showing his irritation with the interruption. 'Ten o'clock tomorrow morning. Downstairs in Reception.'

'What?' Half her attention was on the telephone that still rang in her room, seeming to become more insistent with each ring.

'I'll meet you there,' he added quickly.

'But——'

'You really should go and answer that telephone; whoever it is doesn't seem about to give up.' He took her key out of her hand and unlocked the door for her, pressing the key back into her hand. 'Goodnight, Beth.' He bent and slowly brushed his lips against hers, his eyes dark as he turned her gently and pushed her inside her room, closing the door softly behind her.

Beth stood dazedly just inside the room, one hand slowly moving up to touch her lips where they still tingled from the caress of Marcus Craven's. It had been the briefest of touches, and yet it had been as if an electric shock had coursed through her body. It had been——

Oh, damn, the phone!

She glared at it resentfully as it continued its insistent ringing. Marcus was right—whoever it was seemed very determined.

Her mother...

Oh, God, what had her mother found out that was important enough to ring her this time of night?

CHAPTER FOUR

'WELL, say something!' Katherine demanded impatiently at her continued silence.

Beth sighed, having sat down on the side of the bed. 'What is there to say?'

'What is there...? What...?' her mother spluttered. 'Didn't you hear what I said—Charles is going to name Martin as his heir instead of you!'

She had heard her mother the first time. It didn't seem unexpected to her, in fact it was an obvious move on her father's part if she sat and thought about it logically. As far as her father was concerned she had let him down as a daughter, and now he had no further use for her. She certainly hadn't thought he would want to name her as his heir, had been left in no doubt how he felt about her.

'It's only to be expected, Mu——'

'Not by me, it isn't,' her mother cut in furiously. 'I almost hit Charles when he told me of his plan earlier. I probably would have done if I hadn't known the satisfaction it would have given him!' Beth could imagine her mother's eyes flashing in anger. 'As it is, I told him exactly what I thought of the idea.'

'And?' Beth prompted drily.

'He told me that it wasn't an "idea" at all, that it will very soon be fact!'

Of course it would. Her father would hardly have told her mother of his plans if he had thought for a moment she could in any way thwart them.

'Then that seems to be that, doesn't it?' Beth dismissed without rancour. In fact, she was relieved about the whole thing. She wanted as little to do with her father as he obviously wanted to do with her.

'It most certainly is not,' her mother snapped. 'You don't think I'm just meekly going to accept that, do you? Because I can assure you I'm not! I think you should come home——'

'Mummy——'

'On the first plane available and... What?' her mother barked impatiently as she realised Beth was trying to say something.

She drew in a deep breath, knowing her mother wasn't going to like what she was about to say. 'Mummy, I'm not in the least concerned about being Da—about being his heir.' She still found it difficult to think of him as her father, stumbling over calling him that, finally deciding not to call him anything. 'I'm glad it's all finally over.' And she really felt as if now it could be, knew there would no longer be any tie to her father. And she was so glad.

'It isn't,' her mother bit out tautly. 'I haven't stayed married to your father all these years to have him calmly disinherit you now.'

'But I don't want his money, Mummy——'

'Neither do I,' her mother said with distaste. 'But I don't intend Martin to have it either!'

Martin... Beth had tried so hard not to think of him at all the last few days; it had been vital to her even beginning to enjoy this holiday.

'I think he's probably earned it,' she told her mother bitterly.

'Oh, darling——'

'Forget it, Mummy.' She still felt too raw to talk about Martin. 'I'm really sorry if the news upset you, but please don't be outraged on my behalf; I'm glad to have it all behind me.' And now, finally it just might be. She had no reason now to see her father or Martin ever again.

Certainly not that of duty!

'I actually feel quite light-hearted,' she assured her mother. And she did, feeling as if a heavy weight had been lifted from her shoulders. She had tried so hard to be the daughter her father wanted, had ultimately failed miserably, and now neither of them owed the other anything. She was finally completely free of him.

'And I feel murderous,' her mother informed her needlessly; it was perfectly obvious how she felt about this new development! 'If the two of them think they can get away with this, they're mistaken!'

Beth wished her mother didn't feel quite so volatile about the subject; she wasn't too likely to just drop the subject if that was the case. Maybe that was understandable in the circumstances, but Beth knew she would rather just forget the whole thing.

'Da—Charles,' she amended tightly, 'can leave his money where he wants.'

'Not to Martin,' her mother ground out. 'Never to him!'

Beth felt numb where both men were concerned. 'Can we talk about this when I get back, Mummy?'

'It will be too late then!'

'I doubt that Charles intends dying in the next week or so,' she derided. Yes, she decided, it felt much easier, much simpler, to call him Charles. She had lived without a father most of her life, had known Charles as that only briefly. But he was no real father to her, had never wanted to be, and never would be again.

'That isn't the point.' Katherine was impatient with her again. 'I will not allow him to do this to you—he's already done enough.'

More than enough, that was why she wanted no further part of him. 'It's up to you what you do, Mummy,' she told her flatly. 'I can understand how you feel, but I don't want to be involved in it. This particular quarrel is between you and Charles.'

'All right, darling,' her mother sighed. 'I realise why you feel the way you do. But your father has had this coming to him for some time.'

Beth instantly felt misgivings; her mother in full flow was something to behold. 'Had what coming to him?' she prompted warily.

'I'm not sure yet,' her mother said slowly. 'But I'm not just going to leave it.'

Beth felt her uneasiness deepen. 'Please leave it, Mummy.'

'Don't give it another thought, Beth.' Her mother sounded preoccupied. 'Enjoy the rest of your holiday, and I'll see you in about ten days' time.'

'Mummy——'

'I shouldn't have bothered you with this at all,' she dismissed brightly—too brightly for Beth's peace of mind. 'I persuaded you to go on this holiday in the hope you would forget about Charles and Martin for a couple of weeks, and now I've gone and brought it all up again,' she realised self-disgustedly. 'I was just so angry—I'm calmer now,' she continued in that over-bright voice. 'We'll talk when you get back.'

'Mummy——' Too late, her mother had already rung off.

Beth slowly replaced her receiver. She could call her mother straight back, but what good would that really do? She knew her mother well enough to be aware that would achieve absolutely nothing; her mother would simply tell her nothing more on the subject.

But Beth still felt that sense of uneasiness, as if there was more to come. She could go home, of course, get the next plane back to England, as her mother had first suggested she do. But she really had no desire to go back to England just yet, had actually started to enjoy this holiday.

How much Marcus Craven was starting to mean in all that she didn't want to hazard a guess.

The kiss he had given her earlier, just before they parted, came back in full force. It shouldn't have come as any surprise to her, when he had insisted on seeing her back to her room, that he had claimed the time-honoured salute to the end of their evening. And yet somehow it had caught her off balance, her reaction instinctive rather than controlled. And, although she had responded only briefly, she *had* returned the caress.

What would have happened if her mother hadn't telephoned at that moment?

Nothing, she told herself firmly. She had learnt the hard way that she shouldn't trust her instincts, that they let her down when she most needed them.

But her first instinct had been to mistrust Marcus Craven; should she ignore that? She didn't know any more.

She had trusted her instincts three years ago, had ignored her mother's warnings about Charles, had felt almost shy about meeting him again after all those years.

She had spent most of her life living quietly on the Isle of Man with her mother, had received terse birthday and Christmas cards along with a suitable present for her age-group on each occasion every year from her father. She had always written a polite thank-you note in return, and that had been their only contact for all those years. There had been no visits, no telephone calls.

But shortly after she had turned twenty-one it had been different. Her father had telephoned her, asking her to visit him in London. Beth had been so taken aback she hadn't known what to say. Her mother had known exactly what *she* had wanted to say, and yet she had accepted it when Beth's curiosity got the better of her and she arranged to meet her father in London the following week.

She and her mother had lived very quietly on the island, commuting from their home in the south of the island to the boutique they ran together in the capital, Douglas. They had made occasional buying trips to London, but this visit to her father in London was to be nothing like that. Her mother had held her tongue when Beth told her of the invitation, although knowing Charles as she did she must have been sorely tempted to discourage her from going anywhere near him. But as a mother she had realised that Beth had to learn these things for herself, that she couldn't protect her any longer.

Her father had been charm itself. Tall, and, at fifty, still very attractive, his hair iron-grey, his eyes the same inflexible colour of steel. Beth had been bowled over by him from the first.

That first weekend had been spent in a whirlpool of dinner parties and social occasions, and at all of them her father had proudly introduced her to his friends as his daughter.

Always hovering on the edge of their group at these social occasions had been Martin Bradshaw, her father's assistant, smoothly stepping in at her side if her father should be called away anywhere. He was tall and blond, with deep blue eyes set in one of the most handsome faces Beth had ever seen.

It had only been later that Beth had realised that was exactly what Martin was; her father's 'Blue-eyed Boy'!

That weekend had been the first of several visits to her father in London, and on each visit she had met Martin again too, quickly coming to look forward to those visits for that very reason.

Her mother had gently tried to warn her to be cautious where both men were concerned, but it had been too late for that; she was completely charmed by her father and the attention he lavished on her, and more than halfway in love with Martin.

When the invitations to London had become more and more frequent, her father asking that she come and be his partner or hostess at one function or another, she had been so thrilled that she had ignored her mother's warnings, quickly arriving at a stage where she had just wanted to see and be with Martin; and as he was her father's valued assistant she had seen him a lot during those weekends.

But it hadn't been enough; she had wanted more than just the friendship he seemed to offer.

And despite all her mother's concern it had ultimately been she who had made it easy for Beth to move to London!

The boutique they ran on the island had done well—in fact more than well—and now that Beth was no longer a child and dependent upon her Katherine had decided that the time had come to expand into the rest of the world, opening first one boutique in New York, and then one in London too. Katherine had gone herself to take charge in New York, leaving Beth to maintain things on the island. But when they had opened in London several months later it had been easier to leave Beth's assistant in control on the island and take over in London herself.

It had been the move her father and Martin had been waiting for!

She had only been in London several weeks when Martin began to call at the boutique on one pretext or another. She had been deeply flattered, overjoyed when he had finally invited her out to dinner.

Beth still shuddered when she remembered how worried she had been at the time that her father wouldn't approve of the relationship!

That first invitation had led to others, and within weeks she had known she was head over heels in love with Martin.

And her father had known, and approved, of what was going on.

By the time Beth's mother had returned from New York it was to celebrate Beth's and Martin's engagement.

Beth had been so excited that evening, her father throwing a huge party for all his friends and associates. Her mother had seen that excitement and done her best to feel happy for her, to appear approving to all the people who eyed her so curiously; they had all been aware that Charles had a wife somewhere, but this was the first time most of these people had actually seen her.

Beth had been so proud of her mother that evening, of her beauty, the elegant way she dressed, the dark green gown she wore a perfect foil for her blonde hair and green eyes, but most of all Beth had been proud of the way her mother held her head up high and withstood all that curiosity that was directed at her.

Her mother had met Martin for the first time that evening, and Beth had sensed her reservations about him. But she had dismissed the feelings, knowing that her mother was always cautious until she knew someone well. She hadn't doubted for a moment that her mother would come to love Martin once she got to know him.

The wedding had been weeks later, a grand affair, totally suitable for the daughter of Charles Palmer. Beth had walked down the aisle with stars in her eyes, had thought Martin the most handsome man in the world as he waited for her, like a golden Adonis.

To her great relief her father had approved of the marriage, although he had requested, due to the fact that he didn't have a son to carry on the family name, that they keep the name Palmer after the marriage. It had seemed a little unorthodox to Beth; in fact she had been practising in her head for weeks how the name Beth Bradshaw would sound once they were married! But Martin had been agreeable to the idea of keeping Palmer, didn't seem to mind changing his name to hers, and in the end it had seemed a small concession to have to make to ensure her father felt happy about the relationship too; the last thing she had wanted to do was alienate him when she had only recently found him again.

Her mother had looked at her searchingly after the wedding as she and Martin were about to leave for their honeymoon in the Bahamas. 'I just want you to be happy, darling,' she had said worriedly.

'And I will be,' Beth had assured her with glowing happiness.

The honeymoon had been her first disappointment.

There had been no question of their consummating their relationship before they were married; the situation had just never arisen. And yet despite the love Beth had felt for her new husband, and the consideration and love he had always shown her, the physical side of their relationship hadn't brought the joy Beth had expected.

But she had assured herself that sometimes these things took time, needed to be treated with patience and gentleness to bring fulfilment to them both.

Her mother's business had continued to flourish, extending to Hong Kong, the Bahamas, Italy, even that centre of chic, Paris. Beth was pleased for her mother, knew this was what she had always wanted. But her prolonged absences during those first few months of Beth's marriage had meant she hadn't had her mother to confide in the way she would have wished. She could hardly have blurted out, on one of her mother's fleeting weekend visits, that she found the physical side of her marriage more than a little disappointing!

She had also found that she saw less of Martin now they were married than she had anticipated, always seeming as he did to be busy with work. Well, always was possibly an exaggeration, but, as Martin had insisted that as his wife she didn't continue to work but occupy her time as hostess of the apartment they now lived in, she had found that time weighed heavily on her hands.

And then she had found she was pregnant, and life suddenly had a whole new meaning. Martin had been pleased by the news, her father delighted, and she had suddenly found herself cosseted and cared for by both of them, which was a wonderful experience in itself.

Her mother had been so pleased that the marriage was turning out so well, was greatly looking

forward to the birth of her first grandchild, and
Beth had been able to tell by what wasn't said
that until then her mother had feared for her
happiness. Now there could be no doubting the
strength of the bond between Beth and Martin,
and her mother had been pleased for her.

And maybe if Beth hadn't overheard the conversation between Martin and the woman who
had been his lover for the last three years, if the
shock of overhearing that hadn't made her lose
the baby, a son, she would have continued in
happy ignorance for the rest of her life!

She was supposed to have been with her mother
on a shopping trip for the baby that day, but had
felt slightly ill for most of the morning, and by
lunchtime she had known she had to go home
and lie down, assuring her mother that she would
be perfectly well after a short sleep, knowing this
from experience.

She certainly hadn't expected to come home
and find Martin in *their* bed with another
woman!

The couple in the bed couldn't have heard her
entrance to the apartment, so engrossed were they
in each other, the sound of their laughter filling
the air.

When Beth first let herself in she had heard
that laughter with a sinking heart, believing
Martin was entertaining a guest in the lounge,
and hardly feeling in the mood to face anyone
feeling as ill as she did, let alone a business
acquaintance of Martin's.

But to her puzzlement the lounge had been empty, the kitchen too, and she had followed the sound of the laughter to the bedroom she shared with Martin, surprised, but still totally unsuspecting, at the reason for him having taken anyone in there. She had believed Martin loved her—they had only been married for eighteen months, she was three months pregnant with their child; why *should* she have had any reason to suspect that Martin was in bed with his mistress?

The two in the bed had been completely naked, Martin lying on his back, the woman draped across his chest, caressing the cleft in his chin as they laughed together.

One look at Martin's face had been enough to tell Beth that he and this woman had already made love, that this was after rather than foreplay. That dark slumbering look in his eyes, that relaxed set to his mouth after he had made love; Beth knew the expression so well. But she hadn't realised, until that moment, that she had been sharing the intimacy with another woman all these months.

She had wanted to speak out, to let them know of her presence there behind the slightly ajar door, but as they had begun to speak she simply couldn't move.

'What if she comes home and catches us?' the woman, a beautiful redhead of about thirty, purred sensuously. She was a complete stranger to Beth; she would have remembered this woman if she had ever met her. 'I know it's exciting making love in the bed you share with her, but it could prove a little awkward if she were to find us here,' she drawled mockingly.

'It's thinking of the times the two of us have made love here that makes it possible for me to bed the little fool at all,' Martin said with distaste. 'She had the sensual imagination and body of a schoolgirl. I suppose she has filled out a little, in certain places, since she became pregnant, but——'

'So you find your pregnant wife exciting, do you?' Dark eyes flashed, scarlet-tipped fingernails raking down Martin's chest with just enough pressure to cause pain.

'Little cat.' Martin laughed his enjoyment of the movement, taking that slender hand in his to provocatively kiss the fingertips. 'You know damn well I've never found her exciting; pregnancy certainly isn't going to change that. In fact,' he added with satisfaction, 'it gives me a good excuse to end the physical side of our marriage completely. We must protect the baby at all costs.'

The woman's mouth hardened. 'That damned baby has cost us enough already.'

'But once Charles's grandson has been born...' Martin caressed the satiny cheek closest to him '...our future will be assured, my position as father of that grandson established. Charles is only interested in his grandson, has used Beth to provide him with that at least, and I'm sure that once the child has been born I'll be able to persuade him that Beth is no longer necessary to our plans. After a suitable period the two of us will finally be able to be together.'

The tiny uptilted nose wrinkled delicately. 'I hope you don't expect me to look after the brat?'

'Of course not,' Martin derided. 'A nanny can be found for him to start with, and then when he's old enough there is always boarding-school.'

The woman frowned down at him. 'You're absolutely sure it's a boy?'

'Absolutely,' Martin said with satisfaction. 'Beth had tests done to make sure the baby was healthy, and we were told the sex from that. I told her there was some history of heart defects in my family so that she would have it done.'

'And she believed you,' the woman scorned.

He grinned. 'My darling Chloe, Beth believes anything I tell her.'

Beth hadn't been able to listen to any more, had already heard enough to make her nausea imminent and her legs feel weak. She had turned and run out of the apartment, pressing the button for the lift, and, when it hadn't come, escaping down the stairs.

And that was when the blackness had engulfed her and she had fallen, fallen, fallen...

She had lost the baby, of course. There had been a complication with the loss, so that she had almost died too, and when she had woken up and been told that her baby was gone and there couldn't be any more she had wished that she had died. She had certainly had nothing left to live for.

Her father didn't even come to see her, and so she had known Martin had been right in his claim that Charles was just using her; now that he had been told of her inability to ever give him a grandson she was of no further use to him.

Martin hadn't come near her either, and she could well imagine the anger he had felt at having his plans thwarted in this way.

But somehow Beth hadn't cared about their absence, hadn't cared about anything any more, the love she had had for both Martin and her father as dead as the baby she had carried and lost.

Her mother had been the one to take care of her, taking her home from the hospital when it came time to leave, installing her in her own apartment, the only sign of emotion Beth had shown being when her mother had asked if she wanted to see Martin. She never wanted to see him again!

Physically she had healed quickly. And much as she might have wanted to die, to know complete oblivion, to stop the emotional pain, her body had had other ideas on the subject. Yes, physically she had recovered. Emotionally she was scarred beyond healing.

When the divorce papers came she had been shocked out of her lethargy, incensed that Martin was daring to accuse her of adultery. And with a man she didn't even know.

It had to be one of Martin's friends, she had decided, a man with as few scruples as he had proved to have.

She had fought the petition, denied the adultery, but finally her weakened state, and the law, had defeated her, and Martin had been granted his divorce on the grounds of her adultery with a man she didn't even know!

Chloe must have been becoming impatient at being kept waiting, Beth had decided; she could see little other reason for the lying and subterfuge that had gained Martin his divorce.

And so it was finished. Over with. The divorce final several weeks ago.

But Beth would never forget what had been done to her, how she had been used, and then callously discarded when she proved no further use to the two men. She doubted she would ever trust another man again.

And now there was Marcus Craven trying to push his way into her life, a man with as much arrogance as her father and Martin.

She gave a nervous start as a knock sounded on the door, frowning as she went to answer it; surely Marcus didn't have *this* much arrogance?

The waiter who had served them at dinner stood outside the door, a red rose held in his hand, a rose very similar to if not actually the same one which had graced their table during the meal.

Beth's frown deepened. 'Yes?'

'From Mr Craven.' He presented the rose to her. 'To thank you for a wonderful evening.' He spoke carefully, obviously wanting to repeat the message precisely.

Beth slowly took the rose, staring at its perfection, the waiter having silently left when she at last looked up.

Yes, now there was Marcus Craven. And she had no idea what she was going to do about him.

CHAPTER FIVE

'I'M GLAD you decided to join me,' Marcus greeted Beth downstairs the next morning.

She hadn't meant to, had breakfasted on the balcony of her room, lingering over her coffee, hoping ten o'clock would pass and she could forget Marcus Craven had wanted her to meet him then.

But as ten o'clock approached she had become restless, moving about on the balcony, entering her room only to go back outside again. And at two minutes to ten she had finally admitted to herself that she wanted to join him, grabbing up her bag from the bed before rushing from the room, arriving downstairs breathless and bright-eyed.

She had never looked lovelier, her cheeks slightly flushed, her hair lightly mussed by the slight breeze out on her balcony, the green dress with its small white spots looking cool and elegant.

She felt as if she was walking into danger for the second time in her life, but at least this time she *knew* that was what she was doing!

'You promised to show me Venice,' she reminded him, steadily meeting his gaze, willing her pulse to stop racing at how handsome he looked in the pale blue shirt and grey trousers, the shirt partly unbuttoned to reveal the dark hair on his chest. Unfortunately, her pulse wasn't taking the slightest bit of notice of her!

'And I will,' he assured her decisively, taking a firm hold of her arm to guide her out into the sunlight.

Now that she was refreshed from sleep Venice looked different again to Beth this morning, the street-vendors out, most of them selling souvenirs, although there was the odd artist trying to capture the beauty around them. A few of them had almost succeeded, and Beth lingered over studying their work.

'We can see them again when we come back,' Marcus teased softly. 'You won't get to see Venice this way.'

'But it's all Venice,' Beth reasoned. 'I'm in no hurry; I have all week.'

Marcus gave an enigmatic smile, and, while they boarded the river bus that would take them around the canal to the Rialto Bridge, Beth wondered how long he intended staying here. He seemed to do what he pleased, go where he pleased, and she felt sure that if he decided to stay the week then he would do so. She couldn't even begin to think how she felt about that.

They got off the river bus at the Rialto Bridge, going up its steps to stand on its middle, small watercraft of every description beneath them as their passengers viewed the bridge from a different angle.

Over the top of the bridge and behind it were small shops and market stalls, and the two of them lingered at one of these to buy pieces of moist coconut, munching on them as they continued to stroll through the crowd gathered there.

As well as its numerous waterways, Venice was a labyrinth of tiny canals and side-streets, little shops tucked away in unusual places, cafés too, the check-cloth-covered tables outside beckoning temptingly as the day began to grow warmer.

'Shall we find somewhere to eat?' Marcus offered as he saw her linger at one of these places longer than before.

She nodded. 'Just a salad for me—and I mean it this time,' she warned. 'Somewhere cool, if possible,' she added ruefully, starting to feel the heat quite strongly after their walk.

Marcus smiled knowingly. 'Trust me,' he nodded, striding forwards with a purpose now.

Trust him? She wasn't sure any woman would be wise to do that, but as companions went he was knowledgeable and patient. Even when he took her into the slightly untidy restaurant, that was obviously frequented by the local people rather than tourists, Beth had confidence in his choice. And she was right to do so, once again her request for a salad was ignored, and the pasta meal that was quickly placed in front of them was mouth-wateringly enjoyable.

'A week like this and I will have put on pounds.' She sat back, replete.

'I think that might be a good thing.' Marcus frowned at her slenderness.

Beth eyed him beneath lowered lashes. 'You think I'm too thin.'

Good grief, she was actually flirting with the man now! She hadn't done that since...

A shadow passed over her face, dulling eyes that had gleamed with mischief seconds earlier. 'I believe it's fashionable to be slender,' she dismissed abruptly, although she knew she was thinner even than a lot of fashion models.

Marcus sipped the wine he had ordered to accompany their meal. 'I wouldn't have thought you were a woman who went along with the crowd.' He watched her over the rim of her glass.

What did he really know about her? Nothing, she admitted, except that he seemed to find her attractive enough to keep following!

'You're right,' she bit out. 'I'm not.' And she never would be again, she decided with a shudder.

Marcus frowned at her. 'Did I say something wrong?'

Not really, although it disturbed her that he thought of her often enough to have decided what sort of woman she was. Where did he expect this holiday friendship to go, if that was the case? She hardly thought he was the type of man to spend hours of his time with a woman who would ultimately return to her own bedroom and expect him to return to his. And she doubted he had taken that into consideration just now when he made that remark about her not being 'a woman who went along with the crowd'!

'Not at all,' she returned smoothly. 'Thank you for today, but I think I should get back now.'

'Why?'

Beth looked startled. 'Why? Well...' She shrugged. 'Because it's time that I did.'

'What do you have waiting for you back there?'

An empty room. The same sort of empty rooms she had been going back to for six months since she had insisted on returning to her own apartment from her mother's after she lost the baby, much to her mother's disapproval.

She had at least managed to salvage the apartment from her marriage, forcing herself to go back there and confront the demons that awaited her. Martin hadn't seemed interested in moving back into the apartment himself, and as it had been a wedding present from her father she hadn't had too much difficulty holding on to it.

She had tried, so briefly, to talk to her father of the reason for her accident, but he had told her she shouldn't have reacted like a fool, that the other woman didn't matter because *she* had been the one married to Martin, the one expecting his child. With reasoning like that on her father's side it was no wonder her mother's marriage to him had failed!

'Beth?'

For several seconds she looked blankly across the table at Marcus Craven, and then the full realisation of where she was and who she was with returned to her. 'You've shown me some of Venice——'

'But it's only early afternoon——'

'And I've taken up enough of your time for one day.' She smiled with a noticeable lack of warmth, signalling for the bill. 'I'm sure you have relatives, friends, you would like to visit.'

'My family come from Northern Italy,' he instantly dismissed. 'And I thought we were friends.' Her scepticism at this claim must have shown in her face because he laughed softly. 'Acquaintances often become friends,' he reasoned. 'It's a natural progression in the relationship.'

Her head went back, her eyes narrowed. 'And just how far do you expect this relationship to "progress"?'

'I expect nothing except friendship,' he shrugged.

'Don't you?' Beth derided.

His mouth tightened. 'Have I asked you for anything else?'

His type didn't *ask*, she just stopped herself from saying. But maybe she was being unfair to him; he had just been good company today. But he was too handsome, too intelligent, too smooth, to only be interested in being 'good company'.

Until a year ago she had never experienced cynicism; now she viewed everything in that light, was sure, with the exception of her mother, that everyone had an ulterior motive for most of their actions. And she didn't believe Marcus Craven was just wasting his time on her—he expected something back in return.

'Not yet.' Her hand was completely steady as she raised her glass to her lips, nodding her thanks to the waiter as he brought her the bill. 'Lunch in return for your time this morning.' She took some notes out of her bag.

Marcus caught her wrist as she would have thrown the notes down on top of the bill. 'You can't buy everything, you know,' he rasped.

Martin had been bought as a husband for her, her father's money had seen to that, and the only thing Martin had given up, the *only* thing, had been his name.

'That hasn't been my experience,' she said dully, removing her arm from his hand with little effort, turning to pick up her bag. 'I really do appreciate this morning; I don't want you to think I'm at all ungrateful.'

'Do you always deliver an insult with a thank-you?' he bit out hardly.

'I wasn't meaning to be insulting.'

'No?' he frowned disbelievingly.

Beth sighed. She *had* enjoyed her morning with him, and if she hadn't started thinking about Martin and her father she would have thanked this man politely at the end of the day and none of this conversation would have taken place.

'No,' she said heavily. 'I really have appreciated the time you've given me this morning, but there must be other things you need to be doing.'

'I can't think of any,' he told her drily.

They were going round and round in circles here, both of them being as stubborn as the other. 'Then perhaps you would like to walk me back to the hotel,' she compromised. 'I thought I would go to my room and rest for a while.'

He gave a rueful smile. 'The pat on the head with a kick in the teeth?'

'Not at all.' She stood up smoothly, looking cool and attractive. 'It happens to be the truth.' And she would much rather deal with the truth nowadays, no matter how painful it might prove to be.

Then why had she avoided telling her mother about this man last night? But she hadn't lied, she consoled herself, she just hadn't mentioned the fact that Marcus was now in Venice too.

It was even hotter outside now than it had been when they went in to lunch, and the thought of a rest in her cool room seemed even more inviting as they strolled back to the hotel.

'It really is a coincidence, your being in Venice too,' she remarked casually.

'Is it?' Marcus drawled.

She arched dark blonde brows. 'Isn't it?'

'No,' he answered derisively, the sun glinting on the darkness of his hair.

She was supposed to be disconcerted by the admission, she knew that, but nevertheless his honesty did shake her a little. 'How did you know I was coming here?'

He shrugged. 'I telephoned your hotel and asked them.'

Her eyes widened. 'And they told you of my travel plans, just like that?'

'More or less.' He chuckled at her indignation. 'Actually, I told them I was your brother and wanted to make sure your reservations were OK. They seemed happy with that.'

This man's undeniable authority would open a lot of doors to him, Beth felt sure.

She didn't want to ask him why he had followed her here. It was enough that he had. And that he had admitted it.

She was silent for the rest of the walk back to the hotel; what could she possibly say after an admission like that?

She couldn't help wondering what this man did for a living, that he had the money, and time, to simply go where the whim took him. The Danieli was an expensive hotel, Marcus's clothes, even the casual ones he wore during the day, were obviously of good quality. She had earlier dismissed the idea of him being a gigolo, but now she began to wonder just what it was he did do for a living.

If he was a businessman he might even know her father!

Not that she thought for one moment that her father would have had anything to do with these meetings; he had made it perfectly obvious during the last year that she didn't even exist for him any more.

'Do you live in London?' she casually asked Marcus.

'No.'

Very helpful!

He was being deliberately obstructive now. But she couldn't exactly blame him—he was merely giving her what she had given him when they first met: absolutely nothing!

'Are you in business here?' she tried again.

'In Venice? No,' he replied with a shake of his head.

Now she knew how frustrated he must have felt for the last three days; it was very irritating, to say the least.

'Are you in business in England?' she persevered.

'Are we playing twenty questions?' he returned tauntingly, although there was a hardness in his eyes that hadn't been there seconds ago. 'If so, perhaps you wouldn't mind telling me a few things about yourself.'

'I was merely making conversation,' she dismissed irritably because she knew she was getting absolutely nowhere fast with this man. He obviously didn't intend telling her anything about himself until she became more forthcoming about herself!

He shrugged. 'I'm just as comfortable with the silence.'

So was she, normally; he had just roused her curiosity to the point where she felt desperate to know about him. How had he made his money? Had he inherited it along with his Italian grandmother, or had he worked and earned it for himself?

Now she had to become curious about him!

When she was told there was another telephone message for her Beth knew it had to be from her mother. It was going to take her mother some time to get used to the idea of Charles leaving his money elsewhere, and until she did accept it she was going to run around in a complete fury confusing everyone. In some ways Beth was now glad of this holiday, would have hated to be in London with her mother right now. Hopefully the worst of her mother's anger would have faded by the time she got back to London.

'Aren't you going to read your message?' Marcus prompted at her side.

Beth had momentarily forgotten he was there, blinking up at him unseeingly for several seconds. And then she realised he was talking about the piece of paper she still held in her hand with her mother's message on it.

'It could be important,' he prompted.

It could be, but somehow she doubted it. It was probably just her mother letting off steam again.

She unfolded the piece of paper, feeling her legs go weak as she read the message there.

'Beth?' Marcus questioned concernedly as she swayed in front of him. 'Come and sit down,' he ordered, taking hold of her arm to guide her away from the reception area and into one of the comfortable armchairs in the large ornate lounge.

As she sat down the piece of paper fell from her hand and drifted to the floor, fluttering slightly before it settled on the carpet. Beth stared at it uncomprehendingly.

Marcus picked up the paper, glancing at it briefly before pushing it out of sight into his pocket, coming down on his haunches in front of her. 'Beth?' he prompted again softly, taking her chilled hands in his and gently rubbing them in his much warmer ones.

It didn't matter that he had put the note away out of sight, that she could no longer see the words printed on it; she knew exactly what was written there. 'M has announced his engagement to Brenda Carlisle'.

M had to be Martin. And Brenda was the daughter of Beth's father's business partner, and just eighteen years old. Brenda was young and beautiful, and must surely be being used in yet another shrewd move by Beth's father and Martin.

Martin would very shortly be Charles's heir; by marrying Brenda the whole business empire would one day be his.

Not that Brenda wasn't attractive; she was a small vivacious brunette with a mischievous sense of humour. But if Chloe had been in Martin's life before and during Beth's marriage to him Beth had no reason to suppose it was any different now. In fact she was sure that Martin was still with Chloe. And, of all the people Martin could have chosen to marry, it was too much of a coincidence that he had chosen Brenda Carlisle, heiress to her father's business and money.

Beth actually liked Brenda, had found her good fun on the few occasions the two of them had actually met, although she had been a little too young for Beth to have made a good friend of her. She certainly couldn't believe Brenda would be any match for the ultra-sophisticated Chloe!

Did *she* feel pain at Martin's engagement? She wasn't really sure what she felt. She had loved Martin once, but his cruelty to her when and after she had lost their baby had left her in no doubt how he felt about her, had ultimately killed any feelings of love she might have had for him.

'I'll get you some coffee,' Marcus said firmly at her side, going in search of a waiter.

Beth closed her eyes to stop the room from swaying. No wonder her mother had telephoned her so promptly, she obviously knew what this meant too; another naïve and trusting young woman sacrificed for the sake of the Palmer empire.

She would have to go back to England as soon as possible, couldn't let Brenda marry Martin without at least trying to tell her what sort of man he was. Not that she thought for a minute that Brenda would actually believe her; the younger girl obviously loved him and had no reason not to believe he loved her in return. And Martin could be very convincing when he chose to be—Beth would never have believed what he was capable of herself if she hadn't seen and heard it with her own eyes and ears. She couldn't meekly sit back and let that happen to another woman without at least trying to tell Brenda the truth about him.

Marcus was returning to her side now, frowning grimly as she went to get up. 'You aren't going anywhere until you've drunk some coffee,' he announced autocratically. 'And gained some colour back in your cheeks.'

She automatically raised a hand to her cheeks, her skin seeming to burn while her hand felt cold. But she could believe she looked pale; she had just received a great shock. It had never even occurred to her that something like this might happen. Brenda was so young, at least twelve years Martin's junior; the match was ludicrous.

Marcus nodded tersely to the waiter as he brought the tray of coffee, pouring the hot liquid himself, ignoring Beth's protests as he added the sugar. 'You need it,' he told her grimly, standing watch over her as she drank the too-sweet liquid.

Was it so obvious that she had received a great shock? Of course it was, she knew that even as she felt some of the colour return to her cheeks, some of the numbness recede from her limbs. A year since she had lost the baby, her marriage in shreds, and yet the pain just seemed to go on and on. Would it never stop? She blinked back the tears.

'Drink,' Marcus instructed forcefully.

She swallowed the liquid obediently, grimacing as she did so, replacing the empty cup on the tray with a hand that was far from steady. 'I have to go to my room and make a telephone call,' she said abruptly.

'I'll come with you.' Marcus's hand came up under her elbow as she stood up.

'No, I... Thank you for today, Marcus,' she said sincerely. 'I'll never forget that you showed me Venice.'

He frowned. 'That sounds rather final.'

She averted her eyes from his searching ones. 'I really do need to go to my room.'

'I'll take you,' he told her again firmly.

There really was little point in arguing with this man in her weakened state. In the end Marcus would do exactly what he wanted to do, and at the moment she was in no condition to argue with him.

In truth she was glad of his supporting hand under her arm as they walked up the steps and into the lift; she still felt very shaken.

Martin had lost no time in securing his future a second time, in *doubly* securing it this time; he wouldn't have half of the empire now, he would have all of it married to Brenda. She wasn't quite sure where that left the woman Chloe in his life, but that was Chloe's problem—Beth's responsibility towards Brenda was hers!

She stopped outside her room, turning to Marcus. 'I really am grateful to you for—well, for your time this morning, and—just now.' She couldn't quite meet his gaze. 'I'm sorry I made such a fool of myself, but I—I had some rather—surprising news.' She owed him that much of an explanation at least, although she was sure he had already surmised that for himself.

He looked at her searchingly. 'There's nothing I can do to help?'

'No,' she replied chokingly, shaking her head.

There was nothing anyone could do about this inner pain, it just kept ripping her apart, time and time again. Just when she thought she couldn't be touched by Charles and Martin any more they would do something else that hurt her.

Marcus still frowned down at her. 'Was it bad news?'

She swallowed hard. 'Bad enough.'

'Is someone in your family ill? Do you have——?'

'*I'm* not up to twenty questions just now,' she pleaded wearily.

'You are going to lie down?'

Eventually she was sure she would have to. She had a couple of telephone calls she had to make first. But she would eventually have to lie down or fall down.

'Yes,' she answered truthfully. 'I will be lying down.'

'I don't like seeing you like this.' He looked worried. 'There must be something I can do, something I can get you?'

Beth could only guess at what she must look like to have elicited this concern, knew that her eyes would be an even deeper green in her pain, her face waxy white, her lips colourless too. She had seen that reflection herself so often not to know just how ghastly she must look.

She put up a hand and gently touched his cheek, where a pulse beat erratically. 'Nothing,' she assured him gruffly. 'But I appreciate your concern.'

'Damn it, I don't want...Beth!' he groaned hoarsely as he gathered her up in his arms, his mouth claiming hers.

Her defences were already down, her need for human warmth far outweighing any call for caution from her bruised and battered heart.

She returned the kiss, clinging to him, wishing the last three years would just disappear, that she had never visited her father, never met Martin, never known the joy and then utter despair of carrying and then losing her own child. She gave a choked sob at the thought of her darling baby.

'Beth?' Marcus cradled each side of her face, his eyes dark with concern. 'Tell me what's happened. Let me help you.'

She shook her head, swallowing back the tears. 'It's nothing. Please—I have to go. I'm sorry if I've been—difficult.'

She quickly escaped inside her room, leaning weakly back against the door.

She was sure her mother hadn't meant for her to do this, but she had to return home now as soon as she possibly could.

There was some problem with the booking, but she finally managed to get a seat on the following day's flight, putting another call through to her mother straight after that, only to be told by her mother's secretary that she was away on business until the following evening. Beth realised this had to be the reason her mother had left the message at all rather than trying to speak to her in person, that it wasn't the sort of thing her mother would usually have left to the impersonality of a message left on a piece of paper, but knowing it was too important not to let Beth know straight away. Her mother had at least tried to protect some of her privacy by referring to Martin as just M on the message, although she had had to put Brenda's name in full; there was no way Beth would have been able to guess that it was the young girl who was intended as Martin's next bride!

The message, she suddenly realised. She remembered now that Marcus had put the crumpled piece of paper in his pocket...

CHAPTER SIX

'IS YOUR seatbelt fastened? We're about to land.'

Beth opened her eyes to look at the man seated beside her. She hadn't even been surprised when Marcus had boarded the plane with her earlier today, had shown even less emotion when it transpired that they were actually seated next to each other too.

She had almost been able to guess this was what would happen once she remembered he had her message in his pocket. Marcus had been intelligent enough to realise how deeply that message had affected her, to guess that it might be enough to make her return to England by her reaction to it. A simple telephone call, not unlike the one he had made to her hotel in Verona, was all that was needed to tell him of her expected departure the following day.

And, of course, he had been arrogant enough to make that call!

She had spent almost all of the previous evening doing her packing, and, when she had gone to bed, had moved about restlessly as she tried to evade the feeling of heaviness which remembering the heartlessness of the end of her marriage and the cruelty of losing her baby always gave her. The thought of something like that happening all over again, with someone as young as Brenda, gave her the shudders.

Consequently, despite what Marcus might have thought her reasons, she had been so exhausted that she had fallen asleep almost as soon as the plane was in the air.

She straightened in her seat. 'It was never unfastened,' she dismissed, searching about at her feet for her handbag. 'I had better go and tidy myself up,' she announced pointedly, her hand moving to undo her seatbelt.

Marcus stilled the movement. 'I said we're about to land.' He nodded in the direction of the illuminated seatbelt sign overhead.

And he meant literally, she realised with irritation. Had he done that on purpose, out of annoyance for her having fallen asleep for the whole journey? She doubted he was that petty—it really wasn't his style at all—but he hadn't left her much time to tidy herself.

Her hair was so fine that it needed only a quick brush through, her only make-up a fresh coat of lipstick.

'Is that it?' Marcus drawled, his brows raised as he watched her. 'Most women I know take hours to "put on their face".'

Beth gave him a look that implied he must know some pretty ravaged women.

His mouth quirked as he accurately read that look, although he sobered suddenly as a thought occurred to him. 'Is anyone meeting you?'

The question was put casually enough, and yet Beth felt that was only a façade, that he was deeply interested in her reply. The only person she had told of her return today had been her mother's secretary, just so that she could tell her mother when she got back from her business trip. Although she doubted that was the sort of 'anyone' Marcus had in mind. And she had to admit that it had never entered the conversation about whether either of them were already involved with someone else.

'Not that I know of,' she said uninterestedly, turning her attention to the view out of the window, instantly recognising London spread out before her, the plane descending rapidly now.

She was actually glad to be back in England now that the decision to return had been made. The holiday did actually seem to have done what it had been intended to do; she felt stronger within herself somehow. Maybe once she had done her duty, as regarded Brenda, she could actually start to rebuild her own life. She didn't remember feeling this anticipation for the future for a long time, a very long time.

Oh, God, that feeling didn't have anything to do with the man seated beside her, did it?

She gave him a stricken sideways look, convinced in her own mind that he had to be even more unsuitable for her to care about than Martin had ultimately proved to be. And yet somehow just having him here beside her gave her back a confidence she had forgotten she had, a feeling that she could cope with whatever there was to come.

She couldn't actually be coming to care about Marcus, could she?

She had assured herself during the previous evening that it didn't matter, that she wouldn't be seeing him again, and yet she knew she had felt a warm rush of pleasure earlier today when she had realised that was no longer true.

Thank God they were back in London and she could regain some of the cautious sense the romance of Venice seemed to have robbed her of. It would never do to become emotionally involved with Marcus Craven.

Because she had suddenly become aware of her softened feelings towards him her manner was even more stilted as they left the plane and went through to collect their luggage. She raised a sharp protest when Marcus took both her cases and put them on a trolley with his own.

'We may as well get a taxi back into town together,' he dismissed practically.

She frowned, almost having to run to keep up with him as he strode off towards the green area of Customs. She was sure he didn't have anything to declare, but he was just the type of person the Customs officers were likely to stop and search, his arrogance seeming to imply he dared do anything.

But maybe his stamp of authority was even more effective, because they were able to walk out unhindered, booking a taxi outside the ter-

minal with little trouble, Marcus raising his eyebrows at her questioningly when the driver asked
where they were going in London. Beth irritably
gave her address before settling into the back of
the taxi, Marcus at her side.

'My apartment isn't too far away from there,'
he told her.

So? Although she found it hard to believe, if
that was the case, that they hadn't met each other
on a social level before now. Until a year ago she
had socialised quite extensively with her father
and Martin.

'Have you lived in London long?' she asked
casually.

'I don't live in London at all,' he drawled. 'I
have an apartment there. I also have one in Hong
Kong and New York. In fact, I've been in New
York for most of the last couple of years or so.'

Having lived in the business world of first her
mother, then her father, and eventually Martin
too, Beth was quite used to this jet-set way of
life. It was also obvious to her that Marcus must
know of her father even if he didn't know the
man himself.

'What sort of business are you in?' She tried
not to sound too interested in his answer.

'Property, mainly,' he dismissed, his eyes narrowed. 'Do you work?'

Now why did she have the feeling that he asked
that question almost scornfully; did she have the
look of someone who had never worked a day in
her life? If so, it was a completely erroneous

impression! But then, Marcus really knew very little about her, as she did him.

'Yes, I work,' she answered stiltedly. 'I manage a clothing boutique.'

Dark brows rose slightly, but he added nothing more to the subject.

Beth felt relieved when they got into town, the drive to her apartment made in minutes then. She just wanted to get settled back into her home, somehow contrive to at least talk to Brenda, and then get on with her life. She didn't know yet whether that would involve seeing Marcus again or not.

He climbed out of the taxi after her when they arrived at her apartment building. 'I'll help you in with these.' He took control of the cases.

'I...' She wanted to object, but the truth of the matter was if Marcus didn't help her upstairs with her luggage she would probably have to make two trips. 'Thank you,' she accepted awkwardly.

His mouth twisted derisively, as if he knew exactly what she was thinking.

They stopped outside her apartment door, Beth reluctant to allow anyone into the home that she had removed any reminder of Martin from and decorated during the last year to suit her own taste. The apartment was her, her home now, restful colours like greens and golds and pastel blues in the different rooms; she wasn't sure she was ready for any man to enter that private world just yet, not even to deposit her luggage!

'Thank you,' she said again, standing her ground defensively in front of her apartment door.

Marcus put down the cases with a wry twist to his lips. 'I'm not going to suddenly leap on you if you invite me inside,' he mocked.

She felt the heat in her cheeks, but otherwise remained emotionless. 'You have the taxi waiting,' she reminded him, opening her bag as she realised she hadn't paid for her half of the fare.

Grey eyes were narrowed to steely slits as he watched the movement. 'I hope you aren't going to be insulting.'

Beth looked up at him warily, seeing the warning in his eyes, slowly releasing the money she had been about to take out and thrust into his hand, closing her bag again with a firm click. 'Thank you for all your help today,' she said instead.

'I haven't been trying to be helpful,' he drawled. 'I know where you live now, so I can call on you again soon.'

'But——'

'Beth,' he derided softly, bending his head to hers, his arms firm as he moulded her body to his.

Her lips flowered beneath his, the warmth flooding her body, her arms moving up involuntarily about his neck, the kiss deepening as his lips explored hers, his tongue gently probing.

She was breathing hard when he at last raised his head, knowing her cheeks would be flushed, her lips red and slightly swollen from his kisses.

Marcus touched one of her burning cheeks with light fingertips. 'I'll see you soon,' he told her gruffly, and then he was gone.

Beth just stood there for several seconds unable to move, and then she gave herself a mental shake. 'Soon' could mean any time in the future, and she had much more pressing matters to deal with.

She was unprepared to find her mother waiting for her in her apartment!

'Darling!' She stood up gracefully from the chair in the lounge as soon as Beth stepped into the hallway, putting down the magazine she had been flicking through. 'I got back late last night and when I called into the office this morning Kay gave me your message about returning today. I wasn't sure what time it would be...' She shrugged.

Beth returned her mother's hug. 'You didn't have to waste your day waiting for me.' It began to dawn on her what a lucky escape she had had; if her mother had met Marcus she would never have heard the end of it!

'It wasn't wasted,' her mother chided warmly. 'Although I'm cross with you for returning at all.' She sobered with a frown. 'There was no reason to cut your holiday short like that, especially when it sounded as if you were having a good time.'

'Martin is engaged to marry Brenda,' she reminded pointedly.

Her mother's frown deepened, her beautiful face only slightly lined, her figure still slim and youthful—although she had confided in Beth that it wasn't naturally so when she was unclothed!

'You don't still care for him, do you?' her mother said incredulously.

'Of course not,' she scorned, putting her cases away in her bedroom. 'But there's Brenda to consider.'

'Brenda?' her mother repeated questioningly.

Beth nodded. 'You did say she and Martin are getting married?'

'Yes...?'

'She's so young, Mummy,' Beth sighed. 'She can't possibly know what she's letting herself in for.'

'She soon will,' her mother grimaced.

'Like I did?' she said pointedly.

'I did try to warn you, Beth,' her mother reminded. 'You didn't thank me for it.'

Because she had been too much in love to want to hear the truth. As Brenda probably was too; she knew better than anyone how convincing Martin could be.

'I have to at least try, Mummy,' she sighed.

'For all the good it will do.' Katherine made a face. 'It won't make you popular, you know. Martin won't like it. Neither will your father, for that matter. I'm sure he feels he's made the best business move of his career. He's been trying to buy Sean out for years; now he won't have to.'

She knew all too well the advantages to her father from his point of view; that was one of the main reasons she was so worried by the match. The other one was Martin himself.

'All the more reason for me to at least talk to Brenda,' Beth said grimly.

'I doubt she will thank you for it either,' her mother sighed knowingly. 'Young girls in love don't, you know.'

'At least my conscience will be clear,' Beth frowned.

'Your father and Martin don't have consciences,' her mother said hardly.

'You don't have to tell *me* that,' she grated.

'No, of course I don't.' Her mother squeezed her hand understandingly. 'Anyway, enough about them,' she dismissed with distaste. 'Tell me about your holiday.'

Marcus Craven...

All the beautiful and wondrous things she had seen, and yet she knew what she would remember most about the holiday was meeting Marcus Craven.

Her mother was watching her with narrowed eyes. 'What happened to the man you met in Verona?' she probed thoughtfully.

Colour flared in Beth's cheeks, and she avoided her mother's gaze, knowing that would instantly look suspicious but unable to do anything else.

'I expect he's back home too now,' she answered evasively.

'And?'

She frowned at her mother. 'And he found the opera as moving as I did.' She shrugged her puzzlement with the question.

God, if her mother ever learnt he had followed her to Venice and then escorted her back to England...! Her mother would be asking him his intentions by now if he had come into the flat with her!

'Is that all he found moving?' Her mother looked disappointed. 'Didn't you see him again after that?'

'Well...yes.' She was reluctant to lie when asked a direct question. 'But holiday friendships never come to anything, do they?'

'A "friendship", hmm?' Her mother settled down comfortably in a chair. 'What sort of friendship was it?'

'Purely platonic, Mother, I can assure you.' She deliberately stopped herself thinking of those nerve-shattering kisses they had shared, several of them only minutes ago.

'Oh.' Her mother looked disappointed. 'So you aren't going to see him again?'

'I don't even know where he lives,' Beth evaded truthfully.

'What a waste,' her mother reproved. 'And he was—interesting, you said?'

'Reasonably.' She deliberately played it low-key. 'But he isn't important now, Mummy. As I said, I doubt I will ever see him again. The main thing now is to see Brenda as soon as possible.'

'Darling, you can't just walk up to the girl and tell her she's marrying the wrong man,' she was warned.

'It's what I feel like doing!'

Her mother shook her head. 'It would just look like sour grapes on your part.'

'She's welcome to him!' Beth said vehemently.

'You see,' her mother grimaced. 'You sound like "a woman scorned".'

'But——'

'As the ex-wife you're bound to be viewed with suspicion, anyway,' her mother reasoned. 'Brenda will just assume you're still in love with Martin and feel jealous of their engagement.'

Beth swallowed hard, feeling ill at the thought of that; the last thing she felt about this engagement was *jealous*. Just the thought of the fate in store for Brenda was enough to make her feel... 'I don't care what she thinks,' she said fiercely. 'If I can't make her see sense then I'll talk to Sean. He may be a businessman, like Charles, but there the similarity ends. And he was always very kind to me when we did meet.'

'He could afford to be then, Beth,' her mother pointed out gently. 'You didn't pose any threat to his daughter's happiness.'

It was starting to sound more and more as if this was going to be more complicated than she had envisaged. But she wasn't going to just leave it, no matter how nasty it might become.

*   *   *

'The Trents are having a party on Saturday. I've already checked that Martin and Brenda will be there, and I've organised an invitation for both of us too,' her mother announced triumphantly.

Beth hadn't been in long from work when she received the telephone call. Much to her mother's disgust she had insisted on returning to work in the London boutique, which she now managed for her mother again, the day after she returned from her holiday.

She hadn't expected her mother to get back to her quite so soon!

'Saturday?' she repeated with a yawn, having instantly tensed at the thought of seeing Martin again, something she had deliberately avoided doing. But she had one more day to get used to the idea. 'You don't have to go too if you don't want to,' she assured her mother. 'I won't be staying long.'

'You hope,' her mother returned drily. 'And I have no intention of letting you, figuratively speaking, walk into the lion's den alone. I let you do it once before——'

'And we both know what happened that time,' Beth finished roughly. 'But Barbara and Alec are hardly lions, and I doubt Martin would dare to make a scene at their home.'

'I never put anything beyond that man,' her mother said grimly. 'I'll pick you up at nine o'clock on Saturday.'

It was easier to just give in when her mother sounded this stubborn, and in truth Beth would rather not go to the party alone. She wasn't frightened of Martin, or anything else he might try to do to her, but it was a long time since she had mixed with those other people on a social level. Then she had been Charles's daughter and Martin's wife, and now she was neither of those things. Now she was her own person—at least, trying to be.

'Unless there's someone else you would rather go with?' her mother asked almost coyly.

Marcus... Her mother had to mean Marcus. He was the only man she had mentioned to her during the whole of the last year.

But of course she hadn't heard from him yet; it was only a day since they had arrived back from Venice. And he was the last person she would want to meet Martin!

'No,' she answered drily. 'Nine o'clock on Saturday it is.'

'Beth——'

'Mummy, I've just walked in the door. My feet ache, and I'm hungry, and——'

'And you don't want to sit there talking to me any longer,' her mother finished wryly.

Especially if it was about Marcus Craven. She was trying not to even think about him, and it was proving more difficult than she had imagined. 'Saturday, Mummy.' She rang off quickly before her mother could question her any further.

She almost fell off the chair when the telephone began to ring again the instant she put down the receiver, snatching it up again. 'Yes?' she barked irritably. Really, after the hectic day she had had, all she wanted to do was put her feet up and eat a leisurely meal.

'Beth?'

All thoughts of relaxing this evening left her at the sound of Marcus's voice so soon after she had been made to think of him yet again!

How had he got her telephone number? What could he want?

'Yes?' Her voice sounded stilted now in her surprise.

'Have I caught you at a bad moment?' The amusement could be heard in his voice.

Any moment would be a bad moment; she was never quite prepared for him. 'I've just got in from work,' she admitted impatiently.

'Alone?'

'Yes—alone,' she snapped irritably. 'I work alone, I live alone——'

'Sounds as if you could do with some company, in that case,' he drawled, as usual unaffected by her curt manner. 'Would you like to go out to dinner?'

'Tonight?' she frowned; all she wanted to do tonight was soak in a hot bath for an hour or so and then curl up in bed with a book that didn't take too much concentration.

'Perhaps not,' Marcus derided, easily picking up on her mood. 'How about tomorrow?'

'Tomorrow is my late night at the shop,' she refused, gently easing her shoes off, at once feeling a little less irritable. In just those few days away she had got out of the habit of being on her feet all day; strolling along at her leisure hardly constituted the same thing, especially when there had been numerous outside cafés she could relax in when she felt like a rest!

'Saturday, then?' he persisted.

She had just made alternative arrangements for Saturday, and she had no intention of breaking them, despite the curiosity she felt about whether or not Marcus would seem as attractive now they were back in London, or whether it really had just been a 'holiday romance'.

'I'm going to a party,' she had to refuse.

'I could go with you,' he instantly offered— as she should have realised he might.

'Er—no, I don't think so,' she grimaced. She was dreading the party enough already, without that.

'I see,' Marcus drawled knowingly, obviously completely misunderstanding the situation. 'Perhaps it would be better if I telephoned you on Sunday some time and we could go through the list of your engagements for next week?'

He was annoyed by her evasiveness, she could tell that. But perhaps Sunday would be a better day for them to talk; the unpleasant task ahead of her should be over by then, and maybe she could start to think of herself and the attraction she felt towards Marcus.

'As far as I'm aware, I don't have any engagements for next week,' she replied coolly. 'So a telephone call on Sunday sounds perfect.'

'But not too early, hmm?' he taunted.

'Sunday *is* the traditional day for lying in.' She deliberately didn't rise to the bait of his mockery.

'I'm not going to state the obvious,' he rasped. 'I'll speak to you again on Sunday.' He rang off with his usual curtness.

Beth put the receiver down more slowly this time, still a little stunned that Marcus had attained her telephone number and called her at all. He *had* meant it about seeing her again soon!

She wanted to see him again; she admitted it, to herself at least.

But she certainly wasn't prepared to see him only seconds after she had entered Barbara and Alec Trent's home on Saturday evening!

CHAPTER SEVEN

As PROMISED, Beth's mother picked her up at nine o'clock on Saturday evening, approving the black cocktail dress Beth had chosen to wear with her hair falling loosely to her shoulders as usual, her make-up attractive, although she had applied more rouge than usual, her cheeks very pale as she dreaded the ordeal ahead of her. Martin could be one of the most unpleasant people she had ever known when thwarted.

'You look wonderful, darling,' her mother assured at her nervousness as they went down to the car, looking very attractive herself in a red sheath of a dress that complemented the tan she had acquired on her travels.

'Ready to take on anything?' Beth derided ruefully.

'You don't have to face him alone,' her mother told her grimly. 'It would give me great pleasure to reduce him to the worm that he is.'

'People like him and Charles bounce back stronger than ever,' Beth sighed, resting back in her car seat with her eyes closed on the drive to the Trents' home.

She had no sooner got in the door to the house, given her jacket to the butler, engaged in polite conversation with Barbara about some trivial matter—although she would guess that her hostess would much rather have questioned her about the divorce and Martin's new engagement —when she saw Marcus across the elegant lounge in conversation with their host!

His devastating good looks in the black dinner suit and snowy white shirt, his air of quiet authority, would have drawn attention to him no matter where he might be, and Beth could see several of the women in the room eye him speculatively, their interest obvious.

But Beth knew she would have seen him instantly anyway, her own attraction towards him undeniable.

'What the hell are you doing here?'

Beth had been so intent on Marcus that she hadn't even noticed Martin's approach until he rasped those angry words in her ear, turning to him with as much control as she could muster given the circumstances. 'Good evening, Martin,' she greeted coolly, looking up at his too-handsome face with the over-charming smile, his body elegantly slender rather than powerful. She couldn't help wondering, after looking so recently at Marcus, how she could have fallen for Martin in the first place!

There were several years' difference in the two men's ages, Martin thirty to Marcus's mid-thirties, and yet it owed nothing to this difference in ages that in comparison with the other man Martin looked weak and affected. Beth knew to her cost that Martin *was* weak where money was in question.

'I asked what you're doing here?' he bit out forcefully, fury glittering in his blue eyes.

'I——'

'Well, hello, Martin.' Katherine joined them, her eyes hard with warning as she looked at him.

Martin never had been quite sure how to behave with Katherine. After all, she was still Charles's wife, even if the older couple had been separated for years. And as usual he obviously felt caught between what he would really like to say to her and what he felt he could in the circumstances. 'Katherine,' he nodded an abrupt greeting.

Green eyes glittered Katherine's contempt for him; she was well aware of his discomfort, and pleased by the situation he found himself in. 'I believe congratulations are in order for you,' she drawled contemptuously. 'And condolences for Brenda, of course,' she added hardly.

'I believe one extends felicitations for the future bride,' Martin ground out tautly.

'Really?' Katherine seemed to consider the suggestion for a few moments, and then she shook her head. 'No, I believe I was right the first time,' she said coldly, giving him a slow scathing look. 'Where is the poor unfortunate girl?'

'Powdering her nose,' he grated. 'But I don't want you——'

'Don't try your little threatening games with me, Martin,' she warned him in a dangerously soft voice. 'I've been dealing with an expert for years, and you aren't in his league!'

'Yet,' he challenged, in no doubt whom she alluded to.

Katherine looked him over slowly, and Beth could only stand back and admire her mother's control; caught off guard as she had been, after seeing Marcus so unexpectedly, she hadn't been ready for Martin's appearance. Her mother had sensed her disconcertion, although she couldn't guess the reason for it, and had taken over the conversation—very successfully, Beth acknowledged with amusement.

'Ever,' Katherine told him tauntingly. 'Oh, I'll admit you're well on your way to being a first-class bastard like he is, but you simply don't have what it takes to really be able to step into Charles's shoes. *Your* success depends on too many other people; Charles succeeded *in spite* of other people!'

'Martin, I... Oh!'

Quite what Martin's reply would have been to her mother's baiting Beth wasn't sure, joined at that moment as they were by Brenda Carlisle, a petite brunette who looked even tinier as she came to stand at Martin's side.

Beth knew the other girl slightly, but she had been away at school when Beth had first joined her father in London, had then gone on to finishing school for a year, and so the two of them had never really had a chance to become friends. And now they never would! At best Brenda would dislike her for trying to interfere, at worst the other girl would hate her for ultimately proving to be correct about Martin.

To say the younger girl was disconcerted at seeing Beth and her mother talking to Martin would be an understatement; she looked absolutely stunned. And Beth could only guess at the stories Martin had related to her about their marriage.

'Brenda,' she greeted smoothly. 'What a beautiful dress,' she said with sincerity.

'Thank you.' Brenda eyed her suspiciously, obviously wary of her motive for being so friendly. 'It's the same colour as—it's one of my favourite colours,' she hastily amended, her cheeks red.

Beth guessed the young girl had chosen to wear the figure-hugging green gown because it matched the colour of the emerald in her engagement ring. She had noticed the engagement ring almost within seconds of the younger girl joining them; her own engagement ring had also had an emerald as its central stone.

Martin couldn't even be original in that, had probably told Brenda that the green of the emerald matched the flecks of green in her brown eyes! He had told Beth the emerald in *her* ring matched the colour of her eyes too...

Her mouth tightened as she turned to Martin. 'I was about to ask you how Chloe is.' She met his furious gaze challengingly. 'But of course it's rude of me to talk of people Brenda doesn't know. Or have you met Chloe?' She looked innocently at the younger girl.

Brenda looked puzzled. 'No, I—um—I don't think so.' She looked completely blank at the mention of the other woman's name.

Beth didn't doubt that she hadn't!

She gave Martin a saccharin-sweet smile. 'You must ask Martin to introduce the two of you,' she told Brenda. 'Or perhaps I could——'

'Brenda, I think we should go and say hello to the Daniels,' Martin cut in forcefully, his gaze glacial as it swept over Beth. 'I trust you'll excuse us?'

'Never,' Katherine answered him hardly. 'But do go and say hello to the Daniels, by all means,' she added dismissively, her expression contemptuous.

'Who is Chloe?' Brenda could be heard asking in a whisper as the other couple moved away.

'I would love to hear his answer,' Beth remarked drily to her mother, taking the opportunity now they were alone to look around the room for Marcus.

He was now in conversation with Barbara, although he was looking straight at Beth!

She nodded acknowledgement of him, her cheeks becoming flushed as he excused himself to cross the room towards her.

'So would I——'

'Mummy, someone is coming to join us,' she hastily cut into her mother's reply. 'Whatever you do, don't talk about Martin!'

Her mother looked surprised. 'But——'

'Hello, Marcus,' Beth greeted softly as he stood in front of her. 'This is something of a surprise.' That had to be the biggest understatement . . . !

'Next week seemed too far away,' he answered softly, his gaze resting briefly on her lips.

But it was enough to make her feel as if his lips had gently touched hers! She couldn't believe the effect this man had on her.

'You said a party,' he continued huskily. 'So I made it my business to find out which party. I took a chance on your coming alone,' he added with a curious look at her mother.

Beth had given up wondering how this man attained the information that he did; just learning to accept that he did was easier than fighting against him!

'This is my mother, Katherine Palmer. Mummy, Marcus Craven.' She didn't add any more about him because she didn't know any more. Only that he kept following her, and she wasn't going to tell her mother *that*!

The two shook hands. 'Of Craven Properties?' Katherine said curiously.

It wasn't surprising to Beth that her mother should have at least heard of him and she hadn't; it was her mother's world, and she was very knowledgeable about it.

'Palmer Industries?' Marcus returned brittly.

'No,' Katherine smiled, not in the least perturbed that he should have made such a mistake; she was used to it. 'You're talking of my husband there. I'm in the clothing business.'

That was a huge understatement of the successful business her mother ran!

'You and your husband aren't in business together?' Marcus had turned on all of his charm now, his teeth very white against the darkness of his skin as he smiled down at Beth's mother.

'Don't tell me you're the old-fashioned type of man who doesn't believe in a woman having a business of her own?' Katherine taunted, not at all insulted by his assumption.

Marcus shrugged. 'Charles Palmer is a well-known businessman.'

Katherine smiled. 'I'm quite well-known myself in my own field. The last thing in the world I would want is to be successful because of who I'm married to.'

'And how about you, Beth?' Marcus turned to her with a speed that took her slightly off guard. 'Have you found success because of who your parents are?'

She frowned at what seemed to be an unwarranted attack. 'It depends what you mean by "success",' she answered slowly, wondering what she had said to cause that narrowing of his eyes.

But as quickly as that harshness in his manner seemed to have occurred it was brushed off again, Marcus once more his charming self as he smiled at them. 'Of course,' he dismissed. 'I should have realised who you are immediately.' He was talking to her mother again now. 'The similarity between the two of you is unmistakable.'

Katherine glowed at the compliment. 'I don't know how the two of you know each other, but I'm glad you do,' she grinned. 'My ego can stand hours of this!'

Marcus raised dark brows. 'Beth and I met in Italy.'

Katherine turned to her, her expression clearly saying, *This* was the 'interesting man' she had met in Italy?

Beth gave a barely perceptible shrug of her shoulders. What could she possibly have told her mother about a man like Marcus Craven without her mother jumping to all the wrong conclusions?

As she was probably going to do now!

And she knew her mother well enough to realise that she wouldn't rest now until she was told everything that had happened in Italy.

'Verona?' her mother queried lightly—too lightly!

'And Venice,' Marcus nodded.

Katherine gave Beth a wide-eyed accusing stare before turning back to Marcus. 'What a coincidence that your schedules should have crossed in that way, not once, but twice,' she mocked.

'Not at all,' Marcus drawled smoothly. 'I don't believe in that type of coincidence.'

He was virtually admitting to her mother that he had followed her round Italy; didn't he realise the assumptions her mother would make from that?

'Or coincidences like tonight,' Katherine teased.

'I've already explained that's the last thing tonight is. Now, can I get you two ladies a drink?' he offered politely—just as if he hadn't given her mother enough information to have her questioning Beth half the night!

'I think I need one,' Katherine said drily.

'Beth?'

'Just wine for me, thank you,' she accepted heavily, knowing by the sardonic twist to his lips that he was well aware of what he had just done; weren't mothers the same the whole world over?

'Beth——'

'Not now, Mummy,' she quickly fended her off once Marcus had gone to get their drinks. 'I'm not here to discuss Marcus,' she reminded grimly.

'Why not?' Her mother gave a dreamy smile. 'He's the most interesting man I've met in years.'

'I told you he was,' Beth replied vaguely, searching the room once again for Martin and Brenda. At least they hadn't left while she and her mother had been talking to Marcus; they were among a group of people on the far side of the room, although Brenda kept giving her surreptitious glances. Poor Brenda, she obviously sensed Beth was a danger, in some way, to the happiness she had so recently attained.

Beth's mother waved her hand about dismissively.

'But you didn't tell me all the other things about him,' she sighed reproachfully. 'The man is a walking—well, he's damned attractive,' she amended impatiently.

'That's all too obvious.' Beth still watched Martin and Brenda. For all that Martin looked his usual controlled self he also kept giving her occasional glances, as if he was still worried in case she should cause a scene.

'*You* think he's attractive, don't you?' her mother prompted enthusiastically.

'He's—interesting,' she conceded again. 'Mummy...' she sighed at her mother's disappointed expression. 'I have to deal with the more immediate problem of Martin before I can even start to think about—well, about anyone else.'

'Oh, damn Martin,' her mother scowled. 'It's time you started to think of yourself a little.'

'Maybe after I've helped Brenda,' she said.

'In the meantime you're going to let a man like Marcus Craven get away!'

'Get away from what?' she repeated incredulously. 'I hardly know the man, Mummy.'

'But he obviously wants to get to know you a lot better, and——'

'Here we are, ladies.' Marcus handed them their glasses of wine, and Beth shot him a sharp look, wondering how much of their conversation he had heard. Not too much, she hoped! 'To a brighter future,' he toasted, his gaze fixed steadily on Beth.

Her mother looked very pleased by this turn of events, smug even, and Beth knew she was going to have trouble with her after this evening. If not before...

'Would you both excuse me for a moment?' She was going to have to run the risk of leaving her mother alone with Marcus for a few minutes while she attempted to talk to Martin and Brenda again. 'There's someone I have to see,' she explained, ignoring her mother's impatient glare, making her way over to where the other couple stood. 'Martin,' she drawled, feeling no satisfaction when Brenda visibly tensed at his side.

Martin's fingers tightened on Brenda's arm, causing her to gasp a little.

'Nick, Mandy,' Beth greeted the man and woman who had been talking to the other couple. 'How are you both?'

'Very well,' Nick replied abruptly. He was a business associate of Beth's father. 'Darling, we must go and talk to Sheila,' he added smoothly to his wife. 'Nice to have seen you again, Beth.' He nodded a curt dismissal.

She felt sure it was no such thing, left in no doubt about how most of her father's and Martin's friends felt about her after the marriage break-up; she had suddenly become socially unacceptable to the majority of them. It was just lucky that Barbara and Alec Trent were more her mother's friends than theirs.

Martin gave a sigh of barely repressed anger. 'What do you want now, Beth?' he rasped between gritted teeth. 'You're making this all very unpleasant for Brenda. Our relationship is over; can't you just accept that?'

The damned nerve of the man, trying to give the impression she still wanted him!

'With heartfelt thanks for my lucky escape.' She nodded grimly. 'I didn't actually want to talk to you at all, Martin,' she told him dismissively. 'I wanted to ask Brenda out for coffee one day. I'm sure we have a lot to talk about.'

'Stay away from Brenda,' he warned harshly.

'I'm sure Brenda is perfectly capable of answering for herself,' she told him pointedly, looking at Brenda as she spoke. 'Unless you already have her so cowed that she can't speak for herself?'

'Of course I can speak for myself,' Brenda rose indignantly to the challenge. 'And I really can't see that we have anything to say to each other, Beth. You were married to Martin, it didn't work out, and now we're going to have a life together. You have to let go, you can't go on humiliating yourself in this way. I realise you didn't want the divorce——'

'Oh, I wanted the divorce,' Beth scorned. 'I just don't like the way it was achieved.'

'Then you shouldn't have betrayed . . . Oh, this is so silly,' Brenda said irritably. 'Martin and I are in love, we're going to be married, and you'll just have to accept that.'

Beth gave a regretful sigh. 'I wish I could, but I know—— '

'Your moment's up.' Marcus suddenly appeared at Beth's side, looking at them all with raised eyebrows as they seemed struck dumb by his interruption of what had been an intensely personal conversation. 'Am I interrupting something?' he finally drawled mockingly.

Beth was the first to recover, shooting her mother a pleading look, only to have her shrug regretfully at having been unable to stop Marcus joining them.

'Not at all.' Beth turned back to Marcus. 'There are always so many people one must talk to at parties, aren't there?' she excused.

He gave a nod of his head. 'Aren't you going to introduce us?' He looked pointedly at Martin and Brenda.

God, that was the last thing Beth wanted to do! But she didn't really have any other choice now that he was standing here. How to go about it without making things extremely awkward, that was the thing.

'Marcus, this is Brenda Carlisle and her fiancé Martin Bra—er—Palmer.' She winced as she had to amend Martin's surname to the one he had chosen to take rather than the one he had been born with. 'Martin, Brenda, this is Marcus Craven.'

The two men shook hands. 'Craven,' Martin acknowledged abruptly.

'Palmer,' Marcus returned, giving Beth a curious look. 'Any relation?'

She moistened dry lips. 'Er——'

'None whatsoever,' Martin put in grimly, turning to Brenda. 'We really should be going, darling.'

Brenda gave him a loving smile before turning to Marcus. 'Nice to have met you. Beth...' Her voice cooled noticeably.

'I'll call you,' Beth hastily told the younger girl before they could leave.

Martin turned back sharply. 'Brenda is going to be busy with the arrangements for the wedding over the next few weeks,' he rasped warningly.

'Not too busy for a girlish chat over a cup of coffee, surely?' Beth persisted derisively.

Martin drew in a furious breath, controlling his temper with difficulty. 'We'll see,' he grated, his movements agitated now as he hustled Brenda towards the door.

Marcus watched him with narrowed eyes. 'Strange chap,' he murmured, shaking his head as he looked at Beth. 'Sorry, I believe they were friends of yours.' He grimaced at his lack of manners.

'Not particularly,' she muttered, desperately wanting to change the subject. 'It really is nice to see you again,' she said huskily, surprised herself at how true that was.

'Is it?' he mocked. 'I wasn't sure what sort of reception you were going to give me.'

She was more pleased to see him than she cared to think about. But the scenes with Martin had left her drained, with the start of a throbbing headache at her temples. She looked around for her mother, frowning when she couldn't see her anywhere.

'She had to leave.' Marcus guessed who she was looking for, smiling as Beth turned back with wide, enquiring eyes. 'I assured her I would take you home.'

Her mother was the absolute...! Beth knew damn well her mother didn't 'have to leave' at all, that this was just her idea of matchmaking. Marcus didn't need any help in that direction, was perfectly capable of manipulating situations to suit himself.

'I can easily get a taxi,' she offered, knowing very well that she wouldn't be allowed to do that, Marcus obviously had an ally in her mother, would get all the help he needed from that direction.

'I don't think so,' Marcus drawled without force, also knowing it wasn't even a possibility. 'Are you ready to leave now?' He looked about the crowded room with narrowed eyes. 'Parties like this aren't really my idea of enjoyment.'

But he had been so determined to see her again, on his terms, that he had put up with the inconvenience of the party!

'Mine neither,' she admitted, her own reasons just as strongly motivated, although not in the same way.

Marcus took a firm hold of her arm. 'Then let's make our excuses and go.'

Beth could only guess at the curiosity that would be engendered by their leaving together, at the gossip there would be once they had left the house.

Barbara Trent eyed them curiously as they approached her. 'Leaving already?' She sounded genuinely disappointed, her smile bright as she looked at Marcus. 'You come to London far too seldom now, Marcus,' she reproved. 'I was absolutely delighted when you telephoned this morning. What brings you back to England this time?' The look she shot Beth said she thought she might be able to guess who it might be.

There was no answering smile from Marcus. 'It's a family matter,' he bit out tautly.

'Oh.' Barbara looked surprised at his harshness. 'Well, do come and see us again soon, won't you?'

Beth laughed softly as they went outside. 'I think you just destroyed all Barbara's illusions of a big romance brewing.'

Marcus unlocked the door to the dark green Jaguar parked at the end of the driveway, opening the door for Beth. 'Really?' He looked puzzled by the claim. 'Surely as far as the people in there are concerned we've only just met?' He got in the car beside her.

'Yes, but—well, you know what gossips are,' she dismissed. She couldn't fully explain to him without bringing Martin into the conversation. And she had no intention of doing that.

'No,' Marcus frowned. 'What are they?'

She shook her head. 'It isn't important. Do you need instructions to where I live or——'

'I think I can remember the way,' he drawled with a twist of his lips.

She felt sure he could, settling down comfortably in her seat, Marcus driving with complete familiarity and confidence. The way that he did everything, Beth mused to herself, watching him from beneath lowered lashes. His face looked harsher than ever in profile, his eyes narrowed as he concentrated on negotiating the traffic. Beth didn't doubt for a moment that he would take her home with little difficulty, despite having been there only once before.

She was starting to believe this man could do anything he set out to do.

Was she *falling in love* with him?

She gave him a startled look. Surely not. She couldn't love any man, ever again, it hurt too much.

But she could choose not to love him.

Did one have a choice when it came to loving someone? She had a feeling not. What...?

'Comfortable?'

She gave a self-conscious look in his direction. Marcus was already out of the car and at her side with the door open, waiting for her to get out. She had been so deep in thought she hadn't even noticed that the car had stopped!

'Very,' she ruefully acknowledged his teasing as she stepped out on to the pavement. 'Would you like to come up for coffee?'

'I thought you would never ask,' he drawled.

Actually, she was nervous of being alone with him after the chaotic thoughts she had just been having about him.

She looked at her apartment with critical eyes as they entered, mentally nodding her approval of the elegant comfort she had introduced into the rooms in the last year. It was a large apartment for one person, she realised, but she had managed to eliminate all trace of Martin. She had a feeling that after tonight Marcus could be the dominating presence she felt here...

'Coffee,' she said decisively, more than a little surprised when Marcus followed her out to the kitchen. She had always believed it was a fairly spacious room, but it suddenly seemed dwarfed. Her movements were sure from habit as she prepared the percolator, looking up at Marcus enquiringly as he suddenly grasped her wrist.

'What's he like?' He frowned down at her hand, his thumb rubbing over her fingers.

She swallowed hard. 'He?' God, surely Marcus couldn't be another man who was just trying to do business with her father and was getting to him through her? It would explain his earlier determination. But she just couldn't bear it if that was the case!

Grey eyes held her gaze unwaveringly. 'The man whose ring you wore,' he said softly.

Colour darkened her cheeks, her mouth suddenly dry. 'How did you—know about that?'

'It always leaves a mark.' His thumbtip slowly caressed the finger that had worn her plain gold wedding band and the emerald engagement ring.

She straightened defensively. 'It was over—long ago,' she dismissed harshly, wondering what he would say if he realised Martin was the man she had been married to. She could see Martin for exactly what he was now that she wasn't blinkered by love, and she didn't want Marcus to know the extent of her folly. 'It isn't important,' she shook her head.

'You've been married,' he said pointedly.

'But I didn't try to hide it from you,' she reasoned. 'You just didn't ask. And I didn't tell you.'

'You reverted back to the name of Palmer,' he said flatly.

Beth drew in a sharp breath, having no answer for that accusation, not without going into details about the name change. And she had no intention of doing that.

'Look, Marcus, I was married—very briefly—and it didn't work out. There's nothing more to be said about it.' She was more vehement than she would have wished to be because of her recent encounter with Martin. 'Now, if that bothers you I—— Oh!' she gasped as Marcus's mouth came down on hers.

All the fight went out of her, as it normally did when Marcus took her in his arms.

His lips were punishing as she clung to him, possessing hers again and again, her pulse leaping, her body all heated fire, her limbs shaking.

The kisses went on and on, Beth feeling as if her body were melting, becoming a part of Marcus, so much so that she could only stare up at him dazedly when he finally raised his head.

A nerve pulsed in his cheek, his eyes almost black.

'*That's* how much it bothers me,' he bit out harshly, turning on his heel and walking out of the room, the door closing softly behind him seconds later.

Beth was left unsure of just *how* it affected him—with a potful of bubbling-hot coffee that no one was going to drink...

CHAPTER EIGHT

BETH sipped from the mug of hot coffee that she held in her hands, her eyes heavy from lack of sleep.

It had been a long night, her thoughts going round and round. She had been wrong about the coffee—she had drunk the whole potful! The mug of coffee in her hand was from a fresh pot she had just made.

She didn't know what had happened last night, had gone over and over it in her mind a thousand times, and she was still no nearer knowing whether her marriage to Martin had bothered Marcus—and, if so, in what way—or not. Had he been showing contempt for that marriage? Dislike of its existence? Indifference? What? She just didn't know.

Just as she didn't know whether or not she would be seeing him again.

Her shattered nerves jumped as the telephone began to ring, and she swore softly to herself as she spilt hot coffee over her fingers, swearing again as the hot liquid landed on her bare toes.

She slammed the mug down on the worktop, hopping across the room to snatch up the telephone receiver. 'Yes?' she snapped.

'Well?' her mother asked eagerly.

Beth frowned, licking the sticky coffee from her fingers. 'Well, what?' she said irritably, massaging her burnt toes now.

'You don't sound very happy, darling.' Her mother seemed puzzled.

'I've just spilt hot coffee all over myself in my rush to answer the telephone, so perhaps that has something to do with it!'

'Oh.' Her mother sounded flat.

'Sorry,' Beth excused her bad temper with a sigh. 'As you said, I'm not feeling too happy this morning.'

'No Marcus?'

'No Marcus, what?' Her irritation was still with her.

'Oh, dear,' her mother groaned regretfully. 'What went wrong?'

'After your masterful piece of matchmaking, you mean?' Beth derided. 'Mummy, subtlety passed you by years ago.' She gave a rueful smile, starting to relax a little.

'Didn't he take you home?' Disgust edged her mother's voice.

'Yes, he escorted me home,' she answered evenly. 'But he also left again, if that's going to be your next question.'

'Beth!'

Her mouth twisted with amusement. 'Don't pretend to sound shocked, Mummy,' she teased. 'Because we both know your next question was going to be "why did he leave?".'

'Certainly not... Oh, all right,' her mother sighed at the truth of that. 'Maybe that would have been assuming too much,' she accepted. 'But he's gorgeous, Beth. I don't know how you could resist him.'

'What makes you think I did?' she returned drily.

'Oh.' Her mother sounded speculative now. 'But if you didn't resist him, and he isn't still there—Beth?' There was a frown in her voice.

'Marcus, it would appear, is something of a gentleman,' she said self-derisively. 'He is also somewhat bothered by the fact that I've been married—and obviously divorced.'

'Why?' Her mother sounded puzzled now.

Why? She wished she knew! She had spent *hours* pondering the same question.

'I mean, it isn't as if it's an unusual occurrence nowadays,' her mother added slowly. 'A man of Marcus's age would be very hard pushed to find any woman who hasn't been involved, in some way, in a serious relationship that has gone wrong.'

'That doesn't mean he has to like it, Mummy,' Beth grimaced.

'But the marriage break-up wasn't your fault, darling. Given a choice——'

'But I wasn't,' she sighed. 'And Marcus isn't comfortable with it.'

'Beth, the man followed you from Verona to Venice, and then back here; I can't believe he finds it that difficult to accept,' her mother scorned.

'Perhaps he hadn't realised then,' she shrugged. Although he had said last night that wearing a ring for any length of time left a mark that was visible; that must surely have been just as visible in Italy...

'Maybe not,' her mother accepted. 'But I really wouldn't have believed he was a man that narrow-minded, especially if he knows none of the circumstances for the break-up.'

Neither would Beth, but he had said he had a partly Italian family, so maybe that had some bearing on his views. If he knew of Martin's reason for divorcing her, the fact that she was no longer able to give him children, his sympathies might lie with the other man anyway! Children were very important to a lot of men, and Beth would be far from the first wife discarded for just such a reason. Marcus was probably also a man whom children would be very important to.

'It doesn't matter, Mummy——'

'Of course it matters!' her mother snapped. 'I'm not going to let Martin and your father continue to ruin your life. If they——'

'That's another thing that bothers me about last night,' Beth frowned. 'What if Marcus decides to accept my failed marriage and then finds out that Martin, a man he was told was no relation to me whatsoever, was actually my ex-husband?' She hadn't realised what a problem that could be until those wakeful hours last night. But it could become an insurmountable one.

'That's Martin's problem——'

'No, it's mine,' she insisted.

'Darling, I think you're facing problems that may never arise,' her mother soothed. 'Going out with the man doesn't mean you immediately have to start making grand confessions!'

'But——'

'It isn't as if you're about to marry the man,' her mother teased.

Beth blushed in spite of herself. 'No, of course not,' she said awkwardly. 'I just—I would feel better if I had been honest about things from the beginning. But Martin——'

'Darling, you just have to forget about Martin,' her mother sighed.

'I would love to, Mummy,' she said wearily. 'But I have a feeling he isn't going to let me.'

She was right about that, wasn't altogether surprised when he arrived at the apartment later that morning, although she was absolutely furious that he dared to use his key to just walk in unannounced!

Beth had had a bath, washed and dried her hair in an effort to wake herself up, dressing in denims and a loose top so that she could do her housework in comfort, was actually down on her hands and knees washing the kitchen floor when she heard the key in the lock followed by the closing of the door!

She stood up slowly, the wet cloth still in her hands as she moved tentatively into the lounge.

Martin stood just inside the room, idly throwing the door key up in the air before catching it again and then pushing it inside the pocket of his cords. His expression was challenging as Beth watched his movements with furious eyes.

She made a resolve to have the lock changed first thing in the morning!

Martin had never attempted to come anywhere near the apartment after she left the hospital, and so the change had never seemed necessary before. But she didn't intend this to happen a second time!

'Your key?' She held out her hand, not really surprised when he made no effort to retrieve it.

'Yes, it is, isn't it?' he mocked.

'I'd like it back,' she grated.

'Why bother?' he shrugged, his hands in his pockets now. 'You'll be having the lock changed tomorrow anyway.'

She glared at him, hating him even more in that moment, mainly for being so damned *knowing* about her. And she had once thought him wonderful, even more wonderful than her father. They had both used and betrayed her.

'What do you want, Martin?' she asked coldly.

He didn't answer her immediately, strolling about the room picking up ornaments before putting them down again.

Beth's nerves were at breaking-point by the time he turned back to her, a mocking expression on his too-handsome face.

'You've made a few changes,' he drawled, his tone leaving her in no doubt how he felt about those 'changes'.

'After I sent your things to you?' Beth scorned. 'I didn't want anything here that would remind me of the mistake I made in marrying you.'

His expression was disdainful as he looked at her. 'The mistake was all mine, believe me,' he derided. 'And it's obvious to me that the decor in here now is all your idea.'

'What do you want, Martin?' she repeated steadily, not at all disturbed by his taunting of her taste—as she once might have been.

'Thanks, a coffee would be appreciated.' He deliberately misunderstood the question, dropping down into one of the armchairs, resting the ankle of one leg on the knee of the other one.

She gave an impatient sigh. 'I don't feel any need to exchange social pleasantries with you—and that includes offering you a cup of coffee!'

Martin shrugged. 'I don't suppose I'll die of thirst.' His expression hardened. 'I want you to stay away from Brenda.'

Beth put the damp cloth down. 'Yes?'

'Yes,' he rasped, sitting forwards, all relaxation gone from his taut body. 'I don't want you going anywhere near her again.'

'Are you still seeing Chloe?'

Anger darkened his eyes. 'None of your damned business!'

'Which means you are,' she said without doubt. 'And your affair with Chloe was very much my business!' she bit out tautly. 'I lost my baby, my only chance of having a child of my own, because of your affair with her!' She wished she could control the emotion in her voice, but that part of their marriage break-up would always be painful for her. Because of Martin's affair with Chloe, because of the conversation she had overheard between the two of them, she would never again know the wonder of that life growing inside her, would never hold her own baby in her arms.

'Bitterness is an ugly emotion,' Martin said with distaste.

'I passed bitter long ago,' Beth told him with disgust. 'But I'm certainly not going to stand by and see another young girl used in the same way I was!'

'You lost the baby because you over-reacted to something you saw——'

'And heard,' Beth put in harshly. 'You were in *our* bed, discussing the physical side of our marriage with your mistress, assuring her that the two of you would be able to be together once I'd had the baby, that then I would no longer be necessary to your plans!'

He looked taken aback that she had heard quite so much of the conversation, but he recovered well. 'Nosy little parkers never hear any good of themselves,' he said unsympathetically.

'You were in our home, in our *bed*,' she repeated incredulously. 'I had every right to be here.' This was the first time she had ever really discussed this with him, their contact after that day a year ago kept strictly to a minimum, most of it taking place through their respective lawyers.

'Most women wouldn't have stayed to listen to the conversation once they realised what was going on,' Martin dismissed without regret.

'I couldn't move,' Beth defended emotionally. 'I was frozen to the spot in disbelief. Until that moment I had believed you loved me. It was earth-shattering to realise that our marriage was just a power-play to you, a step up the business ladder.'

'So you acted like an immature child and miscarried our son!' he scorned disgustedly.

'Yet another step up the business ladder,' she accused heatedly. 'That's all he was to you too!'

Martin drew in a ragged breath. 'Rehashing the past isn't going to help anything——'

'Are you still seeing Chloe?' she firmly repeated the question.

'Yes!' he answered forcefully, his eyes narrowed with dislike.

'Then the past is still very important to this situation,' she breathed heavily. 'Especially to the young girl you're about to marry.'

His hands clenched into fists at his sides. 'Interfere with my relationship with Brenda and I'll——'

'Yes?' Beth challenged as he hesitated about making the threat.

'Don't do it, Beth.' His voice was dangerously calm, all the more effective because of that.

She felt a shiver of apprehension down her spine, but remained outwardly unmoved. 'People like you and Charles have to be stopped,' she told him quietly.

'And you intend being the one who does it?' Martin sneered. 'You're way out of your league, Beth, and likely to get hurt.'

She gave a harsh laugh. 'You can't hurt me any more than I already have been.'

'Don't you believe it,' he grated.

If she had been out of her league with these two men, how much more adrift Brenda must be!

'I'm not going to back down, Martin,' she told him firmly. 'Brenda is only a child; someone should at least try to protect her from you.'

'You don't even know her,' he snapped.

'I know her well enough to realise she doesn't deserve you—I don't think any woman does. Except possibly Chloe,' she added with distaste.

His mouth twisted. 'Brenda won't be unhappy as my wife.'

'Why not? I was!' Beth snapped.

His expression was mocking. 'No, you weren't,' he taunted. 'Admit it, Beth, until you overheard that conversation between Chloe and me you had been completely happy with me.'

'That isn't quite true,' she scorned. 'You see, I was no more happy with the physical side of our marriage than you were.'

'That's a lie——'

'No, Martin, it's the truth. But I just thought that side of our marriage wasn't quite so important as the fact that I loved you. But even that happiness was based on lies, *your* lies.'

His eyes were narrowed with dislike. 'You were happy, Beth, believed in me totally. Brenda will have no reason to doubt that belief.'

'Until she's served her purpose,' Beth derided. 'And then she'll be discarded, as you intended I should be!'

'Stay out of this, Beth,' he warned her again hardly.

'Or else what?' she challenged.

'Or else I won't be answerable for the consequences,' he rasped, standing up to move to the door. 'Stay away from Brenda, Beth,' he repeated softly. 'I don't intend letting anything, or anyone, ruin things for me this time.'

'I'm not going to go away just because you want me to,' she told him huskily, wishing he would leave now, her confidence starting to develop serious cracks in the face of his continued insolence. 'And I'm not going to keep quiet either. You need to be stopped, and I'm going to attempt to do it.'

His hand cupped beneath her chin as he looked down at her. 'Perhaps you should have shown some of this spirit when we were still married; it makes you look quite beautiful.' He laughed softly as she wrenched away from his caressing hand. 'You've been warned, Beth.' His voice hardened, his eyes narrowed. 'Don't say you weren't. I don't feel kindly disposed towards people who choose to thwart me.'

The trembling she had known inside ever since she began to challenge him became more tangible once he had left the apartment, and she clasped her hands together to stop it. She had appeared quite defiant to him, she could tell that by his continued warnings, and yet the reality of it was she was shaking in her shoes at the prospect of going against Martin and her father. She knew what they were capable of better than anyone, and she could quite well believe that Martin meant his threats. But she wasn't going to let another woman's life be ruined by him, especially when she might be able to do something about it.

She gave a nervous start when the doorbell rang almost immediately; but at least Martin seemed to have heeded her warning about using his key. But what could he have forgotten to say to her the first time? It had felt as if he had said it all!

'Marcus,' she greeted thankfully, her relief like a warm tide washing over her as she saw he was the one who stood there. 'Oh, Marcus,' she choked her relief, almost falling into his arms.

He held her close against him, his chest solid reality. 'What is it, Beth? What's happened?' he demanded concernedly.

She couldn't tell him, clinging to him until the shaking began to subside.

'I saw Palmer leaving as I came in; does he have anything to do with this?' His voice was gruff, still holding her against his side as he moved into the apartment and closed the door behind him.

She stiffened, straightening away from him. '*Martin* Palmer?' She pretended surprise.

'Yes.' Marcus was watching her with narrowed eyes.

She moistened her lips. 'Did he see you?' she asked as casually as she was able.

'We said hello to each other, if that's what you mean,' Marcus shrugged, casually dressed in blue trousers and a pale blue shirt, the shirt unbuttoned loosely at the neck.

The fact that the two men had seen each other was enough. How was she supposed to explain Martin's presence here at all, especially after her reaction to Marcus when he had first arrived?

'What did he want, Beth?' Marcus's eyes were narrowed questioningly.

What could she say? If she lied again about her relationship to Martin she would just be digging herself deeper and deeper into the subterfuge, and if she continued to see Marcus the truth was sure to come out at some time. Most of the people at the party the previous evening had been aware of the fact that she and Martin were ex-wife and husband; it would only need one casual remark from someone for Marcus to be made aware of that too. And considering the amount of interest that had been engendered about herself and Martin the previous evening she didn't think it would be too long in coming.

But how to tell Marcus, that was the problem.

She moistened dry lips. 'Marcus, I think there's something you should know.' She paused, searching for the right words. It had to sound *right*, somehow.

'Yes?' He watched her agitated movements with narrowed eyes.

'Martin is—was——'

'Yes?' Marcus prompted again as she hesitated awkwardly.

'Last night,' she began again, trying another method, 'you mentioned the fact that I had reverted back to my maiden name after my divorce.'

He shrugged. 'But you were right, a lot of women do that. When there are no children involved it seems ridiculous to live with an everyday reminder of a mistake you've made— and paid for.'

He had obviously been doing some thinking about it since last night! That was reassuring, but it still didn't make this any easier.

'The thing is...' she swallowed hard '...I didn't. Revert back to my maiden name, I mean. I never changed my name in the first place,' she explained in a rush. 'It's always been Palmer.'

Marcus frowned, her faltering explanation really doing little to explain anything.

'When I married,' Beth paused again, sighing, 'my husband changed his name to mine, not the other way around!' There, she had said it.

She watched Marcus anxiously, waiting for realisation to dawn, as she was sure, with a man as intelligent as he was, that it ultimately must!

He looked at her questioningly, shaking his head as he seemed to find no answer there, starting to slowly pace the room, glancing at her every now and then as he frowned in thought.

Beth felt at breaking-point, the tension almost unbearable. But this had to be done, no matter what her mother felt to the contrary. She had to be true to herself, as well as Marcus.

Marcus came to a sudden halt across the room from her. 'Martin Palmer is your husband,' he said slowly.

'Was,' she corrected sharply.

'Was,' he repeated tersely, his expression giving away nothing of his feelings at the realisation.

'You see, Martin told you we weren't related to each other,' Beth rushed into speech as his silence continued. 'Which was true. But after that it would have been extremely difficult for me to have said, "Actually, we were once married to each other".'

'You had the closest relationship any man or woman can have,' Marcus rasped.

'In a successful marriage, perhaps,' she conceded. 'Ours wasn't.'

'We talked about your marriage after that; wouldn't it have been better to have explained then?'

'I wish I didn't have to tell you any of this at all,' she said emotionally. 'The marriage was—a disaster. And it's never pleasant to have to admit to one's mistakes.'

'Why was he here this morning?'

Something else she would rather not have to explain; telling the truth seemed to be a lot more complicated than the initial evasion!

'Our marriage ended rather unpleasantly; last night was the first time we had seen each other for some time.'

'Yes?' Marcus's gaze was compelling.

She shook her head. 'He came here this morning because he seemed to think we had some unfinished business to discuss.'

'And did you?'

'No!'

Marcus frowned. 'I seem to remember he was at the party with his fiancée...'

'That's right,' Beth nodded abruptly. 'He was.'

'A young woman with stars in her eyes,' he said slowly. 'The same young girl mentioned in the telephone message you received in Venice.'

She had forgotten he had seen that message—'M has announced his engagement to Brenda Carlisle' —blushing as she realised how damning her reaction to that news must now seem.

'I must admit, I didn't make the connection last night,' Marcus murmured thoughtfully. 'Why did the announcement of your ex-husband's engagement to another woman make you rush back to England in the way that you did?'

She sighed, wishing he had never seen that message. 'It was—a surprise.'

'Why?'

Her mouth firmed. Really, she didn't have to explain herself to anyone. And yet she could see how damning this must all look to Marcus.

'Why was he here today, Beth?' Marcus persisted at her lack of a reply. 'Is it not over between the two of you, is that it?'

'Oh, it's over,' she scorned. 'So much so that I think Brenda needs warning!'

'I see,' Marcus nodded slowly.

Beth frowned, not sure that he did at all. 'Do you?'

'I think so,' he grated. 'You know, I had started to seriously doubt the things I had heard about you——'

'What things?' She gave him a startled look. 'What are you talking about?'

'It doesn't matter——'

'It matters to me!' she insisted indignantly. 'What have you heard about me? And from whom?'

'I've said that doesn't matter,' Marcus rasped coldly. 'But you obviously are the spoilt little bitch I was told you were if you feel so vindictive about your ex-husband that you are willing to ruin his new relationship. I take it that was what was meant by "a girlish chat over coffee" with Brenda Carlisle?' he said disgustedly.

Beth was pale at the unexpected attack. 'I wanted to talk to Brenda, yes——'

'And obviously Palmer is aware of exactly what you want to say to her!' His eyes blazed angrily. 'Or perhaps it isn't vindictiveness that drives you,' he scorned. 'Maybe it's jealousy. Do you regret your divorce?'

'No, I——'

He shook his head, not listening to her. 'I can't believe I've been so foolish as to actually start to believe I was wrong about you.' His mouth twisted in self-derision. 'I'm not going to give you the satisfaction of admitting I could actually have come to care about you, because I realise now that's what all your little games were about——'

'Games?' Beth echoed dazedly. 'What games?'

'It almost worked, you know,' Marcus rasped. 'I can't believe I've been so stupid!'

He pulled her roughly into his arms, his mouth punishing on hers as he ravaged her mouth without mercy.

Just as suddenly he thrust her away from him, his gaze raking over her with complete contempt before he turned sharply and stormed out of the apartment.

Beth slid slowly to the floor, her legs too weak to support her...

CHAPTER NINE

'MR CARLISLE will see you now.' The house-keeper smiled at Beth politely as she waited for her to follow her through to the lounge.

Coming here this evening hadn't been easy for Beth, but she had telephoned Brenda several times and tried to speak to her, and the younger girl had consistently refused to even take the calls. Beth felt she had been given little choice but to contact Sean Carlisle himself.

She knew Sean, of course; a big bluff Scotsman, with flaming red hair and a smile that could lull business rivals into a false sense of security concerning his ability. But he wasn't her father's partner for nothing, and if he could maintain his side of that relationship without sacrificing his own principles then he could attempt anything.

He looked a little embarrassed as she came into the room, crossing the lounge to shake her hand. 'Nice to see you again, Beth,' he said gruffly.

'Is it?' she doubted ruefully, sympathising with his awkwardness. It couldn't be every day he received a visit from his future son-in-law's ex-wife!

Sean shrugged. 'You're Charles's daughter; of course I'm pleased to see you. I'm not quite sure of the reason for your visit, but...'

'I'm not only Charles's daughter, I was married to Martin,' she grimaced.

'Ah,' he nodded.

'That's what you were afraid of, hmm?' Beth made a face. 'I'm sorry about that.'

'I'm not,' he smiled. 'Sit down, why don't you? I'll organise some coffee for us both.' He rang the bell by the fireplace, a young maid entering seconds later.

Beth sat down. She really wasn't looking forward to this conversation, had a feeling Sean would deeply regret his friendly hospitality before she had finished. If he took her warnings seriously then he wouldn't thank her for the upset she was about to cause; Brenda was the centre of his world, his wife having died years ago.

'Would you like to pour?' he suggested once the coffee tray had been placed on the low table.

Stay out of it, her mother had told her, but the more imminent Brenda's and Martin's marriage became the more uneasy Beth became about it all. She *couldn't* stand idly by.

She poured their coffee. 'I don't think you should allow Brenda to marry Martin.'

Auburn brows rose over warm brown eyes. 'That's pretty blunt and to the point!'

'Sorry,' she grimaced. 'But I don't know of any other way to say it.'

'Oh, I'm not complaining,' he said, holding up dismissive hands. 'Straightforwardness is to be recommended, not rebuked.'

'I hope you still think so by the time I leave,' she told him ruefully.

'Tell me what you have to say, and let's see, hmm?' he prompted gently.

Beth told him everything, leaving nothing out, sparing no one, not herself, not her father, and certainly not Martin. Sean listened without change of expression, occasionally asking the briefest of questions, but for the main part remaining silent.

His very silence made it easier for Beth to talk without being overcome by emotion, but by the time she had finished she was shaking badly.

'What would you say,' Sean spoke slowly a few seconds after she had fallen silent, 'if I were to tell you that, except for actual conversations that took place, none of what you've just told me is a surprise to me?' He frowned.

Beth swallowed hard. 'I would ask why you're letting your daughter marry Martin.' Surely no father could deliberately let his daughter walk into such a marriage?

Why not? Her own father had! But Sean wasn't in the least like her father—was he...?

He gave a rueful grimace. 'Why don't I get Brenda downstairs and let her explain that for herself?'

Beth looked startled. 'Are you telling me that Brenda knows about all that too?'

'I'll get her,' Sean said decisively, going upstairs himself to get his daughter rather than sending a maid.

His absence gave Beth a few minutes to collect her thoughts together. Sean and Brenda actually knew what Martin was like and the young girl *still* intended marrying him? It was unbelievable!

Brenda looked as fresh and young this evening as she had that night almost a week ago, and yet Beth looked at her with new eyes. The face was still slightly freckled, the eyes still a deep brown, and yet there was a maturity in their depths that Beth had never realised was there before. Whatever, Brenda didn't look like a wide-eyed innocent this evening, with stars in her eyes.

'Daddy tells me you've come to warn me against marrying Martin,' she said lightly as she dropped down into an armchair.

No, definitely no wide-eyed innocent today. Beth wondered if Martin knew he had a tigress by the tail. My God, the two of them could even deserve each other. Now, wouldn't that be hysterically funny?

'Do I need to bother?' Beth said self-derisively.

Brenda gave a rueful shrug. 'Not really. Because I love him, you see, "warts and all". I have done since I was fifteen years old, only he married you while still believing I was a child. I could hardly believe my luck when the two of you separated so quickly, and then divorced,' she added without any sign of malice, just stating bare fact. 'I still loved him, you see; nothing had changed for me.'

And Sean was prepared to let his darling daughter have anything, anyone, that made her happy; Beth could see that now. It was all so incredible.

'I do see,' she said slowly. 'I don't understand, but I do see.'

Brenda shrugged again. 'I'm not like you, Beth, I have my eyes wide open about just what sort of person Martin is.'

'And you love him anyway,' she realised dazedly.

Brenda smiled. 'Yes. And to finally answer your question of the other evening, Beth, yes, I do know about Chloe. I also know she's going to be out of his life so fast once the two of us are married that he'll wonder what happened. Our marriage will work, Beth, and on my terms, you'll see.' She spoke with complete confidence.

And she was probably right, Beth realised, because she had the support and power of her father behind her rather than against her as Beth had.

Beth gave a rueful shake of her head. 'I'm almost starting to feel sorry for Martin.'

'Only almost?' Brenda laughed, looking quite lovely, and totally unconcerned about the success of her future.

As well she might! Beth had felt totally despondent about this visit but she had a feeling she might leave feeling somewhat elated, definitely relieved at the very least.

'Yes, only almost,' she admitted drily. 'Are you really sure you want to go through with this, Brenda?' She sobered. 'Martin's never going to change, you know. He came to see me last Sunday to warn me off talking to you again.'

'He isn't the reason I didn't take your calls,' Brenda said gently. 'I just thought it would be easier on everyone if we stayed away from each other.' She stood up. 'I still think that's the best way to handle this because we really can't have any more to talk about. I certainly don't want to compare marriages!'

'Neither do I,' Beth said with feeling.

Brenda nodded. 'Then I had better go and get changed; I'm meeting Martin later.'

Beth watched her leave the room, feeling more than a little dazed, wondering how any woman—for undoubtedly that was what Brenda was, no innocent young girl at all!—could marry a man she knew was untrustworthy before the wedding.

She shook her head. 'If Brenda is fooling herself and really does believe she can change him——'

'She isn't,' Sean assured her heavily. 'She loves him just as he is. I would rather have anyone else as a son-in-law.' He shook his head. 'But he's what Brenda wants...'

And what Brenda wanted, she got. Beth had a feeling Martin had more than a few shocks waiting for him in the years to come.

'It will be different with Brenda,' Sean assured her grimly. 'I know exactly what Martin is after, and how to deal with him. Don't worry, Beth; he won't get away with anything married to my daughter.'

She could see that, felt an enormous sense of relief, as if the whole responsibility had been lifted from her shoulders. She couldn't help thinking Brenda was condemning herself to a lifetime of unhappiness with Martin, but she was doing it wilfully, so what more was there to be said?

Beth stood up. 'There doesn't seem to be anything more to be said.' She shrugged.

'No.' Sean gave a rueful smile, standing up too. 'But I do thank you for your concern, Beth; I know that it couldn't have been easy for you to come here at all.'

'Especially as it turned out to be so unnecessary,' she grimaced.

He gave a gentle smile. 'Your father is a fool; I've told him so on numerous occasions.'

'I'm sure he liked that.' She still found it difficult to talk about her father.

Sean shrugged. 'I've never particularly cared whether he liked it or not. The first stupid thing he did was let your mother go; after that he just compounded things every time he saw her by acting like an idiot. He still loves her, you know.'

Beth gave him a startled, disbelieving look. 'He can't do.' She shook her head.

'But he does,' Sean nodded. 'The only problem is that his ambition and drive are obsessional with him, and even people he loves are sacrificed to that end.'

'I know that better than most,' Beth said with remembered bitterness.

'He's been the loser,' Sean sighed. 'But he always will be, especially while there are people like Martin to benefit from his obsession. But you mustn't worry about that situation any more, my dear,' he said again firmly. 'I'm not without power and ambition myself.'

He would never have survived as her father's partner all these years otherwise, Beth realised. And where Sean's daughter's happiness was concerned he wouldn't hesitate to use his power, just as he wouldn't hesitate to destroy anyone who threatened that happiness. But she knew now that Brenda had a lot of her father's strength and determination, that she would probably never have need of his power, being quite capable of managing her own life in any way that suited her.

She left to go and meet her mother for dinner, although she was still slightly shaken from the meeting with father and daughter.

'She always was a spoilt little minx,' her mother said ruefully when Beth had related the conversation to her. 'I thought the finishing school in Switzerland might have changed all that.'

'And instead her apparent docility is just a trap to ensnare Martin,' Beth said ruefully.

'She sounds just what he deserves,' her mother said with satisfaction. 'Two of a kind.'

Beth nodded. 'They do seem very alike. I just hope Brenda doesn't end up getting hurt in spite of herself.'

Her mother shook her head. 'I doubt it. You'll see, in twenty years' time the two of them will still be married, and Martin will be totally bewildered by it all.'

It conjured up an amusing picture, and Beth couldn't help but smile.

'That's better.' Her mother nodded her satisfaction. 'I've been worried about you the last few days.' She looked at Beth closely. 'Has something happened to upset you?'

Beth hadn't seen Marcus since the morning after the party when she had told him the truth about Martin and he had said those awful things to her. But she had far from forgotten the incident, was still stunned by it. Marcus had spoken as if he had been warned against her, and she couldn't think of anyone—other than her father and Martin, and he obviously didn't know either of them—who disliked her enough to do such a thing. She also wondered exactly *what* he had been told to make him believe such things of her.

But she didn't know where he lived when he was in London, had no intention of embarrassing herself by asking the Trents for his telephone number, and so the situation had remained, as far as she was concerned, unresolved.

'Beth?' her mother prompted at her continued silence. 'You haven't heard anything from Marcus; is that the problem?'

Her mother had no idea the two of them had spoken again after the party, and Beth had no intention of telling her otherwise. That humiliation was better kept to herself.

'Of course not,' she answered sharply.

'Sure?'

'Very,' she replied vehemently to the gentle probing. 'I... He was too much in the same mould as Charles for me to ever feel comfortable with him.' And yet she had enjoyed his company, she knew she had, had been halfway to falling in love with him!

Her mother frowned at this. 'I don't think he's at all like your father in the ways that would affect you.' She said slowly. 'He's capable, yes, very self-assured too, but I don't think there's any cruelty in him.'

Maybe he wouldn't be deliberately cruel, but he had hurt Beth, and he seemed willing to believe his informant about her, whoever he or she might be, rather than giving her the opportunity to defend herself.

'Speak of the devil,' her mother murmured.

Beth looked up sharply, following her mother's gaze across the room.

Marcus had just entered the fashionable restaurant, a younger man at his side, although there was a certain family resemblance in the thick dark hair, grey eyes, and the slender but powerful build. Marcus hadn't mentioned having a brother, only an older sister, and yet Beth couldn't see the younger man being anything but a blood relative of his. A son, perhaps? That was a possibility she had never thought of. If Marcus also had a broken marriage behind him... But even so, that was no excuse for the way he had behaved towards her, especially as he didn't really know what he was talking about.

'He's coming over,' her mother muttered.

Oh, God, now what was she supposed to do? They could hardly be polite to each other after the contemptuous way he had dismissed her on Sunday.

'Katherine,' he greeted her mother politely. 'Beth...' His voice cooled noticeably.

She looked up at him reluctantly, her breath catching in her throat at how handsome he looked in the dark evening clothes. God, he was attractive. How on earth had she managed to resist him in romantic Italy? She hadn't, not in the end!

Delicate colour darkened her cheeks. 'Marcus,' she returned in a quiet voice.

Dark brows rose. 'Are you about to leave or would you rather we ate somewhere else?'

Beth heard her mother gasp but continued to hold Marcus's gaze herself. 'We aren't about to leave—haven't been here long ourselves. And you can eat where you please.' The last came out aggressively as her temper got the better of her. Did he have to make it so obvious he would rather not even eat in the same restaurant as her?

'Katherine?'

'Feel free.' Her mother looked totally bewildered by the whole conversation.

'Very well.' He turned back to Beth. 'As long as you won't find it too embarrassing?'

Her mouth firmed. 'Why should I be embarrassed?' she dismissed flippantly.

He glanced across the room to where the younger man stood, looking slightly bored now, his hands thrust into his pockets as his gaze scanned the room for anyone who looked interesting. 'If you're sure,' Marcus drawled. 'Ross looks slightly impatient for his meal.'

'Then you had better go and feed him, hadn't you?' Beth snapped tightly.

His eyes darkened. 'I have to admire your nerve.'

'Do you?' she returned challengingly.

He nodded. 'No one mentioned that you have guts.'

Beth shrugged, inwardly shaking, but having no intention of letting Marcus see that. 'Maybe your informant wasn't as reliable as you seem to think,' she derided harshly.

'I said it wasn't mentioned, not that it was denied,' he grated.

She glanced past him to his impatient companion, the younger man starting to look very irritated now at being kept waiting in this way. 'Don't let us keep you,' she said coldly.

He gave a slight smile. 'Nice to have seen you again, Katherine.'

His omission of Beth's name was deliberate, and it showed.

The last thing Beth wanted to do now was eat in this restaurant, but there was no way she was going to leave until she had done exactly that. Even if every mouthful choked her!

Her mother looked deeply disturbed once they were alone. 'What was all that about, Beth?'

She shrugged, not quite able to meet her mother's gaze. 'I'm not sure. But I don't think Marcus will be following me anywhere in future!'

'Beth——'

'Could we just forget it for now, Mummy?' she cut in, holding on to her control with difficulty. 'And enjoy our meal?' She smiled up at the waiter as he brought their starters.

Relaxing and enjoying anything was out of the question for her, of course, very upset as she was by the conversation with Marcus, but she somehow had to get through this.

She didn't know what had suddenly turned him against her, she only knew she could feel his antipathy across the restaurant, felt his gaze on her often, refusing to look in his direction herself, knowing her self-control would crumble if she did.

Because she *had* fallen in love with him, not just halfway, but completely!

She had sworn never to love again, had learnt the hard way how painful loving someone could be, and now she had fallen in love with someone even more unsuitable than Martin had been. Marcus actually seemed to hate her; Martin had just despised her!

But she loved Marcus, more than she had ever loved Martin, this love based on experience and suffering the like of which she had never thought to know.

It didn't seem fair that she should love so unwisely a second time, but Marcus had persisted in her life until she could ignore him no longer. And now he didn't even want to know her.

'Are you sure you're all right, darling.' Her mother looked at her worriedly as they came, thankfully, to the end of their meal, Beth's crumbling control noticeable now despite all her efforts to the contrary.

'Shall we go?' Beth gave a strained smile, crushing her linen napkin and placing it on the table.

Her mother frowned. 'Do you want me to have a word with Marcus——'

'No! No,' she repeated less audibly, noticing several heads in the restaurant turning in their direction, Marcus's one of them; he probably thought she was just having a temper tantrum. After all, that was what 'spoilt little bitches' did—wasn't it? 'The less either of us speak to Marcus Craven the better,' she assured her mother with a shudder.

Unfortunately they had to pass the table the two men occupied on their way out of the restaurant. To have left by any other route would have looked as if they were deliberately avoiding going near them, and Beth didn't intend giving Marcus that satisfaction.

Marcus looked at her coldly as they drew level with his table, and it was left to the younger man to give her an admiring glance, the invitation in his eyes leaving nothing to the imagination. Perhaps Marcus had told the other man she might welcome the attention! Although the glare he shot in the younger man's direction didn't seem to imply he approved of the attention he was paying Beth.

His reaction brought out a streak of defiance in her, and she deliberately stopped beside the table, her smile seductive as she looked at the younger man while directing her remark to Marcus. 'You didn't introduce your friend earlier.' Her voice was deliberately provocative.

Marcus looked taken aback. 'This is my nephew.'

'Really?' she pretended surprise, although the family resemblance had been obvious from the first. 'I never would have guessed.' She bestowed a warm smile on the younger man. 'You don't seem at all alike,' she flashed hardly at Marcus, her eyes gleaming cat-like in her slightly flushed face. 'Nice to have met you, Mr Craven,' she told the younger man, her tone implying she didn't feel the same way about his uncle, before she swept haughtily out of the restaurant, her mother at her side.

'That was very good, darling,' her mother murmured. 'Very impressive. But it won't keep you warm at night.'

'Neither will Marcus!' she said abruptly, feeling emotionally drained now, something her mother respected on the drive back to her apartment.

'Do you want me to come in?' her mother offered gently after parking the car.

'No,' she refused heavily, knowing a deep need to be alone.

And yet once she was alone in her apartment it was the last thing she wanted, feeling closed in, unfairly judged, frustrated with that judgement, wanting to know the reason for it, angry with Marcus for so easily accepting whatever it was he had been told about her.

It was the latter emotion that was pre-dominant when the doorbell rang seconds later, and she answered it to find Marcus standing on the doorstep. 'What do you want?' she scorned. 'Have you come to throw more insults at me?' She stood defensively in the doorway, barring his entrance.

'I have to talk to you,' he rasped.

Her brows rose. 'That wasn't the impression you gave earlier.'

'Earlier I was...' He shook his head. 'I have to talk to you, Beth. Now.'

'I don't think I want to talk to you——'

'Beth...' the quiet authority in his voice silenced her '...tonight you met the man named as co-respondent in your divorce. Not only did you not recognise him, but he didn't recognise you either, and you called him by completely the wrong name. Beth, my nephew is Kinross Bentley, the man you're supposed to have committed adultery with, and the two of you don't even know each other. Now I want to know what the hell is going on!'

CHAPTER TEN

BETH swallowed hard. That man, that *arrogant* young man with the knowing eyes and too much self-confidence, was the one Martin had paid to lie about her. Marcus's *nephew*?

'Why don't you go and ask him that?' she dismissed scornfully, a hundred different thoughts coursing through her mind, none of them making any sense. Not yet anyway; she was too stunned for that.

'Because I'm asking you,' Marcus grated. 'I'm not interested in anything Ross has to say.'

'You don't seem to have had any trouble listening to him before!' Because this surely had to be Marcus's informant—a man who didn't even know her!

'And now I want to hear what you have to say,' Marcus said grimly.

'How do you know I'll tell you the truth?' she derided, her head back defiantly.

He shook his head. 'I know damn well that Ross hasn't!'

Beth sighed, stepping back. 'Then you had better come in, hadn't you,' she said dully.

She didn't completely understand the situation herself. How *long* had Marcus known his nephew had been named in her divorce? Did that have something to do with their initial meeting, and the consequent ones? Was that the reason none of their meetings had been a 'coincidence'?

She turned to face Marcus across the lounge. 'Perhaps you had better tell me what you already know,' she told him flatly. 'Or think you know,' she added hardly.

Marcus breathed in deeply, his hands thrust into his trouser pockets. 'I have a feeling, having come to know you as I do, that you aren't going to like it.'

'I'm sure I won't,' she muttered. 'But it has to be said anyway.'

'Very well,' he nodded decisively. 'As you know, I've spent most of the last couple of years in America.'

'It has been mentioned,' she said drily.

'Hmm,' he grimaced. 'Well, while I was there it would seem I neglected my duties as guardian to my nephew Ross.'

Beth frowned. 'He looked young, but not that young.'

Marcus made a face. 'Ross is only twenty, for all he might wish, and act, as if he were older. That was why, when it was brought to my attention, I was horrified at the affair and subsequent naming in the divorce of a woman several years older than he, not only in age but in experience.'

'You mean me?' Beth realised disbelievingly.

He paced the room. 'When I challenged Ross about the affair he told me that you had paid him to be named as co-respondent after your affair ended, that you were willing to do anything to get rid of the husband you had become bored with.'

'That's a lie,' she gasped.

'Let me finish, Beth,' he urged gently. 'Then you can tell me what really happened.'

'How kind,' she was stung into retaliating.

'Beth, this isn't easy for me either—it never is when you realise what a fool you've been.' He looked pained.

As well he might!

'It can't be,' Beth scorned.

'Ross is a very wealthy young man——'

'Then why take the money my *ex-husband* paid him to lie about my adultery?' she accused heatedly. 'If he didn't need the money——'

'As Ross's guardian I have the power to decide whether or not he takes control of that wealth at twenty-one or twenty-five. He's had an allowance for the last three years, since my sister and her husband, his parents, were killed in a plane crash, but it would seem he's been living well above that allowance, that he had debts that needed repaying, the sort of debts that he daren't come to me about,' Marcus added grimly. 'He got in with a crowd that were older than him, that thought nothing of losing several thousand pounds a night in a casino——'

'Martin's crowd,' Beth realised.

'It would seem so,' he confirmed. 'He had debts that needed paying, and he admitted to me that he had accepted money from you to help you get rid of your husband.'

'I didn't divorce Martin; he divorced me—with the false evidence Ross gave him!'

Marcus shook his head self-disgustedly. 'I had no reason at that time to doubt Ross's word. Even the fact that Bradshaw had changed his name to yours after the marriage seemed to confirm you were——'

'A spoilt little bitch,' Beth finished with a sigh. 'That wasn't my idea. As you would have found if you had ever bothered to ask *me* what happened!'

He gave a groan. 'I'm not proud of my part in this.'

She looked at him intently. 'Just what *was* your part in all this? Just exactly why did you go to Italy?'

'To meet the woman who was so determined to rid herself of a husband she was bored with that she was willing to pay someone to go into court and have their name blackened for her,' he admitted harshly.

Beth gasped. 'And?'

'And instead I met a very beautiful woman with an air of vulnerability about her that made me want to wrap her up and protect her from the world!' He shook his head. 'I went to Verona, after discovering that was where you had gone to amuse yourself, with the intention perhaps of intriguing you a little myself, so that you would know what it felt like. Instead I ended up totally

bewildered, by the contrast in the things I had
been told about you, and the ethereally lovely
woman I finally met. It didn't make sense.'

'And so you thought I was playing games,' she
said bitterly. 'Repulsing you one minute, seem-
ingly accepting your company the next.' She
could see it all now, just how damning her own
behaviour must have appeared in view of what
he had been told about her.

'Nothing else seemed to make sense,' Marcus
admitted heavily.

'And now?' she choked.

'Now I think I had better hear the true facts
from you,' he invited heavily.

Beth drew in a ragged breath. Marcus had
sought her out, deliberately, with the idea of
punishing her in some way for her selfish use of
his nephew. What form had that punishment
been supposed to take? Was *she* supposed to fall
in love with him and then be rejected?

If so, he had succeeded!

'The truth isn't only mine to tell,' she spoke
raggedly. 'There are other people involved,
innocent people, who can still be hurt by the truth
if it was to become public knowledge.' She was
thinking most of her mother, her poor mother
who was still loved by a man who ultimately tried
to destroy all those who loved him.

Marcus looked grim. 'I'm not the public.'

'Even so——'

'I *need* to know the truth, Beth,' he almost
pleaded. 'I need to know that very much.'

Why? She looked at him searchingly. What possible difference would knowing all the sordid details of her divorce make to him?

'You owe me that much, at least,' he prompted at her hesitation.

'Owe you?' she repeated forcefully, her eyes shooting sparks of displeasure at him. 'I don't owe you anything! You were the one who sought me out, remember?'

A nerve pulsed in his jaw. 'Please tell me the truth,' he requested softly.

Her cheeks were flushed. 'All right, I'll tell you.' And she did, leaving nothing out, faltering only when she came to telling him about losing her baby and not being able to ever have any more. 'So you see,' she concluded bitterly, 'I'm not the one who plays games; I leave my father and Martin to do that.'

Marcus was completely silent and still, as he had been as she told him the details, his face grey now.

His continued silence unnerved Beth, until she felt at breaking-point, wanting him to go, or stay, to at least *do* something.

'They did that to you?' he finally grated.

'Oh, yes,' she confirmed, without bitterness; there was no point in that, not any more.

'Ross too?' His gaze was compelling.

Her mouth twisted. 'For a price, it would seem, yes.'

'But what he said about—an affair—was false?'

'I've just told you it was,' she scorned incredulously. 'Martin was the first and only man I've—known, in that way.' Her cheeks were flushed with embarrassment. *This* man was the only other man she had ever wanted in that way, and look how misguided that attraction was, even more so than she had originally imagined. 'Remember, it was the fact that your nephew and I didn't even know each other this evening that brought you round here in the first place.'

'Right,' he acknowledged a little shakily, 'You do realise what this means?'

'Oh, yes,' she derided. 'It means my father and Martin are both despicable.'

Marcus shook his head. 'It means much more than that.'

Beth gave him a puzzled look. 'It does?'

'Don't you see, Beth?' He grasped her by the shoulders. 'The evidence given in your divorce was false; worse than that, it was fabricated for monetary gain.'

'I told them at the time of the divorce that it wasn't true,' she defended. 'No one, not even my own lawyer, I'm sure, believed me!'

'I believe you,' Marcus said harshly.

'I could have done with your support then,' she mocked, 'not a year later. Now it does little but give me the personal satisfaction of knowing someone else knows exactly what happened!'

'But, Beth, it's so much more serious than that.' His hands tightened on her arms. 'Your father, your ex-husband, my nephew, all lied to attain the divorce. They all broke the law by giving false evidence. I doubt that your divorce is legal!'

Beth stared up at him in horror before collapsing in his arms in a dead faint.

CHAPTER ELEVEN

FREE.

Beth was a free woman at last, on her own terms, with no black shadow of lies and deceit looming over her.

Marcus had proved correct about the divorce, and so Beth had had the pleasure of divorcing Martin instead of the other way round, all three men receiving the displeasure of the court for their previous deceit. Her father and Martin's subterfuge had become public knowledge, and there could be no doubting that both men had suffered personally for it as well as legally. But they would survive, and, as Beth had known she would, Brenda had stood by Martin.

Then why didn't Beth now feel happier with the truth finally out? Why did her life feel so flat and—without direction?

'This is supposed to be a celebration, not a wake, Beth,' her mother chided teasingly.

Beth looked at the champagne luncheon before her, a glass of the bubbly liquid itself standing in front of her. None of this seemed to matter either.

'Beth, it's all over now.' Her mother squeezed her hand. 'Your father finally got what he deserved and you're free of both him and Martin.

You can now do exactly what you want with your life.'

She grimaced her lethargy with that idea. 'There's nothing I want to do.' She sighed.

'Strange,' her mother murmured. 'I thought there was something—someone—you very much wanted in your life.'

Beth gave her a sharp look, turning away again at the speculation in her mother's eyes. 'I don't know what you mean—— '

'Darling, the fact that you love Marcus has been blazingly obvious for weeks,' her mother put in gently.

'To Marcus too?' she groaned, wondering if that was the reason he had left them so suddenly today once the court case was over.

For weeks he had been there, a quiet but constant support, and then today, when it was all over, he had made his excuses and left without saying whether or not she would be seeing him again.

His duty over? His responsibility as Ross's uncle—Ross having been one of the men to cause her pain—over and done with? She admitted that over the weeks, although there had been nothing said or done, she had begun to hope he might care for her and wasn't just correcting a wrong that had been helped in its success by his ward.

But he had left them earlier, refusing to join them for lunch, despite Beth's invitation for him to do so.

'No,' her mother answered her question. 'The two of you have been hiding your feelings from each other very successfully.'

Beth moistened her lips, her heart leaping with excitement. 'What do you mean?'

'Marcus loves you,' her mother said matter-of-factly.

'No! He——'

'Yes, Beth,' her mother insisted. 'Why else do you suppose he was so supportive?'

'He felt responsible for Ross's part in it.' She shrugged.

'That responsibility was dispatched by providing you with one of the most competent lawyers in the country. I'm having dinner with James tonight, by the way,' she added coyly.

'Really?' Beth smiled. She had liked James Hawthorn from the first, a tall distinguished-looking man in his early fifties.

'Really,' her mother cajoled. 'I may even get around to divorcing your father one of these days.'

Her mother must like James very much to be considering that! Beth was glad. If anyone deserved love and happiness in her life then her mother did.

'Let's get back to you and Marcus,' her mother said firmly, not about to be distracted any further.

'There is no Marcus and me,' Beth dismissed.

'But there could be.'

'I don't——'

'Marcus is just being honourable, I'm sure,' her mother insisted. 'The last eighteen months have been hell for you, not least because of his nephew's part in it. How can Marcus now turn around and tell you how he feels about you? The poor man is in a very awkward position.'

'You don't know how he feels about me——'

'I know that he had fulfilled his obligation to you by initiating the sorting out of the legal tangle his nephew had helped get you into by providing James to help you. He didn't have to continue visiting you, spending time with you, coming with you today. He's a busy man in his own right, and yet he's spent weeks——'

'All right, Mummy,' Beth ruefully silenced her. 'You have me convinced that Marcus over-stepped the lines of obligation. But that doesn't mean——'

'Why do you think the whole thing was so important to him?' her mother demanded impatiently.

'His nephew——'

'Oh, damn his nephew!'

'Mummy!' She frowned at her mother's vehemence.

'Darling, men like Marcus do not involve themselves in what is, after all, a family matter.'

'Marcus does; that was why he followed me out to Italy in the first place,' she said stubbornly.

'Oh, stop being so pig-headed, Beth,' her mother rebuked impatiently. 'It isn't going to do

you any harm to go and thank the man
personally——'

'I've already thanked him!'

'Will you stop interrupting me?' Her mother
sighed irritably. 'When did you get to be so
stubborn and——'

'Pig-headed, I know,' Beth laughed softly. 'I
just don't think——'

'For once in your life don't stop to think,' her
mother instructed. 'Follow your intuition and go
and see Marcus. You have nothing to lose——'

'And possibly everything to gain,' Beth finished thoughtfully. 'Maybe I could just go
and——'

'Go.' Her mother took her untouched glass of
champagne out of her hand. 'Now. I'll see to the
bill.'

Beth shook her head ruefully. 'Try looking in
the mirror some time if you want to see where I
get my stubborn pig-headedness from.' She stood
up as Katherine pulled a face at her. 'I'll see you
later.'

'Don't hurry back,' her mother called after her.

It was fine saying she was going to see Marcus,
something else to actually do it. Oh, she knew
where he lived now when he was in London, had
been to his apartment several times during the
last few weeks—purely on business matters, of
course.

Beth didn't give herself time to change her
mind, to hesitate, going straight from the restaurant to Marcus's home, smiling confidently at

the doorman, knowing that within seconds of her stepping into the lift Marcus would know of her imminent arrival, via a discreet telephone call made to his apartment.

She didn't even know what she was going to say to him, had no idea——

The apartment door was flung open before she could even ring the bell, and she found herself pulled roughly into Marcus's arms, pressed against his hard chest, breathing in a smell that was a pleasure to her senses, part Marcus and part the aftershave he wore.

'I was just on my way to join you at the restaurant after all.' His chest rumbled as he spoke huskily. 'I got back to my apartment and just sat here wondering when I would be able to see you again. Beth, the idea of never seeing you again was slowly killing me,' he breathed deeply into her hair. 'I can't believe you're here!'

He did love her; her mother had been right!

'Marcus.' Her hands came up to cup either side of his face. 'I think we may both have been being very stupid these last few months. I love you; I have done since Venice.'

Fire burned in his eyes. 'I think I fell in love with you when I saw your tears in Verona,' he admitted gruffly. 'I had expected to see a hard, brittle woman; what I found was a delicate butterfly who looked as if life itself were hurting her——'

'I was horrible to you that first night——'

'I deserved it; my only defence is that I thought I was dealing with a totally different type of woman entirely. And that's no excuse! Beth, I——'

'Marcus, let's get out of this hallway.' She looked about them self-consciously. 'We really can't make love out here!' she teased shyly.

He looked about them dazedly, as if he had been momentarily unaware of their surroundings, grimacing ruefully as they went inside, although he sobered suddenly. 'We aren't going to make love at all,' he told her softly. 'If you really do love me——'

'I've been in love with you for weeks.' She smiled indulgently at his lack of confidence. 'You only had to give me an indication of how you felt and we could have been together long before now.'

'I couldn't have been that close to you and not made love to you.' His eyes were dark with desire.

'You wouldn't have had to be.' She caressed the hardness of his cheek with gentle fingertips.

'Beth, I love you, and I don't intend making love to you until after we're married... What is it?' He frowned darkly as she moved abruptly away from him. 'Beth?' He looked strained.

She moistened her lips. 'I can't *marry* you, Marcus——'

'I realise your experience with Bradshaw must have put you off marriage,' he grated. 'But it won't be like that between us.'

'I know it won't,' she assured him shakily, knowing without a doubt that it wouldn't, her faith in him unshakeable, her response to him undeniable. God, how she wished she could say yes, but she knew she couldn't. 'But I can't marry anyone.'

'I'm not asking you to marry anyone, I'm asking that you marry *me*.' Marcus still frowned, looking like a man who had been dealt a blow.

'Marcus, I can't——'

'Why?'

She swallowed hard at the harshly asked question. 'I told you I lost the baby; that I can't have any more children——'

'And you think that bothers me?' He turned her roughly to face him, his hand beneath her chin as he forced her to look at him. 'I want *you*, not any children we may or may not have from our marriage. Who's to say *I* can give you children——?'

'You could be tested——'

'Would you feel any differently about me if I were; if we found I couldn't give you children? Would it stop your loving me?' he demanded.

Her cheeks were flushed. 'No. But——'

'But nothing, Beth. I want to marry you; nothing less will do. If we decide we would like children then we can always think about adopting them——'

'Your Italian grandmother would turn over in her grave at having you marry someone who can't give you children,' Beth said harshly.

'There are already enough grandchildren in the family; I have no inclination to add to their number. All I want is you, Beth.' He held her arms as he looked down at her. 'For a lifetime. I've never had children, so I won't miss them if you decide adoption isn't for us, but if you go out of my life for a reason so unfounded, on any level, then my life will be flat and——'

'Without direction,' she finished knowingly. 'Oh, Marcus, I do need you,' she groaned, tears brimming in her eyes. 'I have a feeling I always will!'

He gathered her close in his arms, kissing her gently, savouring the caresses, controlling the situation for both of them.

'I love you very much, Beth,' he finally murmured huskily.

'And I love you,' she answered unhesitantly.

And it was all that mattered, all that would ever matter.

Love. And Marcus. A lifetime romance.

OVER THE YEARS, TELEVISION HAS BROUGHT
THE LIVES AND LOVES OF MANY CHARACTERS INTO
YOUR HOMES. NOW HARLEQUIN INTRODUCES YOU
TO THE TOWN AND PEOPLE OF

One small town—twelve terrific love stories.

GREAT READING...GREAT SAVINGS...
AND A FABULOUS FREE GIFT!

Each book set in Tyler is a self-contained love story; together, the
twelve novels stitch the fabric of the community.

By collecting proofs-of-purchase found in each Tyler book, you can
receive a fabulous gift, ABSOLUTELY FREE! And use our special
Tyler coupons to save on your next TYLER book purchase.

Join us for the fifth TYLER book,
BLAZING STAR by Suzanne Ellison, available in July.

Is there really a murder cover-up?
Will Brick and Karen overcome differences and find true love?

BIG SUMMER READ

Summer Reading At Its Best

In July, Harlequin and Silhouette bring readers the Big Summer Read Program. Heat up your summer with these four exciting new novels by top Harlequin and Silhouette authors.

SOMEWHERE IN TIME by Barbara Bretton
YESTERDAY COMES TOMORROW by Rebecca Flanders
A DAY IN APRIL by Mary Lynn Baxter
LOVE CHILD by Patricia Coughlin

From time travel to fame and fortune, this program offers something for everyone.

Available at your favorite retail outlet.

BSR

Harlequin Presents®

Coming Next Month

Available in July wherever paperback books are sold, or through Harlequin Reader Service:

In the U.S.
P.O. Box 1397
Buffalo, NY
14240-1397

In Canada
P.O. Box 603
Fort Erie, Ontario
L2A 5X3

Take 4 bestselling love stories FREE

Plus get a FREE surprise gift!

Back by Popular Demand

A romantic tour of America through fifty favorite Harlequin Presents, each set in a different state researched by Janet and her husband, Bill. A journey of a lifetime in one cherished collection.

In July, don't miss the exciting states featured in:

Title #35 OHIO
The Widow and the Wastrel
#36 OKLAHOMA
Six White Horses

If you missed your state and would like to order a copy, send your name, address, zip or postal code, along with a check or money order for $3.99 (please do not send cash), plus 75¢ postage and handling ($1.00 in Canada) for each book ordered, payable to Harlequin Reader Service to:

In the U.S.
3010 Walden Avenue
P.O. Box 1325
Buffalo, NY 14269-1325

In Canada
P.O. Box 609
Fort Erie, Ontario
L2A 5X3

Please specify state with your order.
Canadian residents add applicable federal and provincial taxes.   JD-JUL2

HARLEQUIN Temptation

Rebels & Rogues

Brew: He'd fought his way off the streets . . . but his past threatened the woman he loved.

THE BAD BOY
by Roseanne Williams
Temptation #401, July 1992

All men are not created equal. Some are rough around the edges. Tough-minded but tenderhearted. Incredibly sexy. The tempting fulfillment of every woman's fantasy.

When it's time to fight for what they believe in, to win that special woman, our Rebels and Rogues are heroes at heart. Twelve Rebels and Rogues, one each month in 1992, only from Harlequin Temptation. Don't miss the upcoming books by our fabulous authors such as JoAnn Ross, Ruth Jean Dale and Janice Kaiser.

FREE GIFT OFFER

To receive your free gift, send us the specified number of proofs-of-purchase from any specially marked Free Gift Offer Harlequin or Silhouette book with the Free Gift Certificate properly completed, plus a check or money order (do not send cash) to cover postage and handling payable to Harlequin/Silhouette Free Gift Promotion Offer. We will send you the specified gift.

FREE GIFT CERTIFICATE

ITEM	A. GOLD TONE EARRINGS	B. GOLD TONE BRACELET	C. GOLD TONE NECKLACE
# of proofs-of-purchase required	3	6	9
Postage and Handling	$2.25	$2.75	$3.25
Check one	☐	☐	☐

Name: _____

Address: _____

City: _____ Province: _____ Postal Code: _____

Mail this certificate, specified number of proofs-of-purchase and a check or money order for postage and handling to: HARLEQUIN/SILHOUETTE FREE GIFT OFFER 1992, P.O. Box 622, Fort Erie, Ontario L2A 5X3. Requests must be received by July 31, 1992.

PLUS—Every time you submit a completed certificate with the correct number of proofs-of-purchase, you are automatically entered in our MILLION DOLLAR SWEEPSTAKES! No purchase or obligation necessary to enter. See below for alternate means of entry and how to obtain complete sweepstakes rules.

HP3C

FREE GIFTS WITH PURCHASE — ONE PROOF-OF-PURCHASE
To collect your fabulous FREE GIFT you must include the necessary FREE GIFT proofs-of-purchase with a properly completed offer certificate.

(See inside back cover for offer details)